D1531614

AND
PHILIPPA
MAKES
FOUR

AND
PHILIPPA
MAKES
FOUR

Martha Derman

FOUR WINDS PRESS
New York

Manufactured in the United States of America

10 9 8 7 6 5 4 3 2 1
The text of this book is set in 12 pt. Garamond.

Library of Congress Cataloging in Publication Data
Derman, Martha.
And Philippa makes four.
Summary: Sixth-grader Philippa feels her life becoming
intolerable as her widowed father becomes romantically
involved with a fellow architect, who is also the mother
of Philippa's school enemy, Libby.
[1. School stories.   2. Family problems—Fiction]   I. Title.
PZ7.D444An 1983   [Fic]   83-1631
ISBN 0-590-07905-0

To Hessy

AND
PHILIPPA
MAKES
FOUR

Part I

AT ABBA AND POP'S

1

"No, no," yelled Philippa in her sleep. Horns seemed to honk, and she was tumbled from her box sled. She tasted snow.

Crash. Philippa jerked awake from her snowstorm dream, the one in which she was three years old again and her mother disappeared behind ambulance sirens.

Tinkle. Real glass clinked in the street.

Philippa sat up and brushed away a lock of hair, glued into a corner of her mouth. She heard footsteps cross the porch. Relieved, Philippa knew her father was home. He'd been out to dinner . . . the Latin teacher again? She looked at the glow dial of her clock. Twelve o'clock. He'd had a long time to eat.

His steps creaked on the stairs. "Dad?" Philippa called.

"I could never be a burglar," her father said.

Philippa started to smile and then stopped. She could not get the sound of breaking glass out of her head.

Shivering a little, Philippa knocked at the bathroom door where her father had the water running. When he opened the door, Philippa saw he held a washcloth to his forehead. "You're hurt!" she said.

"I bumped my head on the rearview mirror when I drove into the maple tree. It was the dumbest thing—my mind was on business, not the driveway."

"I'll put a Band-Aid on it," said Philippa. She pushed back a shock of his hair, the color of her own except for a streak of gray at each side.

"I went with the Jolliffes and a friend of theirs to look at a building downtown—ow, there's a bruise under there —and we got to talking afterward. Thanks, Flip. You'd better hustle into bed."

Philippa huddled in her rumpled bed. It was so cold for September. A branch scratched at the siding as if to come in. Her clock hummed like a live thing.

She hid her head under her pillow. She wondered if Abba and Pop had heard the crash. Her grandmother and grandfather had a rear room on the first floor. Pop, who had a bad leg, was not supposed to climb stairs.

A reassuring sound came among the creepy house noises—click-click-scratch over the floorboards between scatter rugs. A cold nose pressed into her cheek. Her grandfather's Labrador knew when you needed him. Philippa patted the bed. "Come up, Jack." Jack heaved himself onto the cold space at Philippa's feet, settling warm as toast on her toes.

Abba had to holler up the stairs twice the next morning. Groggily, Philippa splashed water on her face. Her towel slid off its rack. She left it on the floor.

There was a snarl in her hair. She brushed a cover-up lock over it. "Rush and fuss, Abba," she muttered, but after she wriggled into her sweater and corduroys, she remembered to sprinkle fish food into the tank by the window. If the guppies did not get fed, they fed on each other.

There was a scraping at her window screen; Frisk, the gray squirrel that Jack chased every time he had a chance, was asking for breakfast. Philippa fumbled three peanuts from her underwear drawer and left them on the outer sill.

"Phil-lip-puh!" The third time. Socks and sneakers in her hand, Philippa ran downstairs and into the kitchen.

"Morning, Abba. Morning, Pop." She pulled on the socks and ignored a hole in one toe.

Her grandmother, called "Abba" since Philippa's baby days, stood tall and stately in a plaid housecoat. "Your cereal is growing cold," Abba said.

Philippa's gray eyes expressed disgust. "You know I hate oatmeal."

"It's so good for young growing things."

"Hea'ing he?" Meaning me? said Pop. Pop's speech had been slurred by a stroke long ago. Philippa had never heard him talk like other people. He carried a little pad of paper in his breast pocket for writing long sentences, but Philippa understood him most of the time.

"Eat up, G. H.," said Abba. "It's good for you, too. Is your father up? I think he came home late last night."

Apparently, her grandmother did not know about the crumpled fender, and Philippa did not want to be the one to tell her. Mouth full of oatmeal glue, she mumbled. "On't 'oh."

Abba sighed. "George is out so much. He ought to get married again."

Philippa's spoon splashed in her dish. "*I* don't want him to get married again."

When her grandmother went to the foot of the stairs to listen for shower sounds, Philippa put her unfinished bowl on the floor and toed it toward Jack. She heard his slurp-slup with satisfaction. Pop grinned at her. Philippa gulped orange juice and then scooped up her books calling, "Bye, Pop. Bye, Abba. I got my lunch money, thanks," as she slammed out the front door.

By the curb, Laurie Coombs, from up the street, gazed at the battered fender and broken headlight of the car. "What happened?" Laurie said.

Philippa shrugged. She dug at a splinter of glass in the bark. "There's that jerko Albert. Let's go so he doesn't try to walk with us." Philippa crossed the street walking backward. She saw Albert pick something yellow out of the gutter.

"Hey, Ja-ane," called Laurie.

Crossing at the end of the block was a procession of

Overrackers, Jane Overracker in the lead, with Denise, Amber, and Ted clustered close around her.

"What's Amber crying about?" asked Laurie.

"She didn't want to walk with the rest," said Jane, "but I can't keep track of everybody and get 'em to school on time if anybody wanders." Jane's mouth was set as straight as the bandanna headband that held her blond hair in place.

Amber's voice broke as she said, "I'm telling Mindy you borrowed her jacket."

"So tell. It's too small for Mindy." Jane waved her hands in fingerless gloves. "Keep moving." She stamped one moccasined foot. The ravelings on the hem of her skintight jeans swirled over the sidewalk. Philippa wished Abba would let her clothes get that great hand-me-down look, but Abba did not approve of Jane's clothes. Nor did Abba approve of Putney Street, the down-at-the-heels street where the Overrackers lived, one block from the Catlett house. Abba even felt that Jane did not take enough baths and would never allow Philippa to invite Jane to stay overnight. Abba and Philippa sometimes had ferocious arguments about that, and the thought of those arguments put Philippa's teeth on edge.

Albert distracted her. He galloped up with a rectangle of yellow plastic held to one eye. It was the parking light from the Catletts' right fender! He squinted through it at Jane. "You're yellow," he said.

"Butter's better," said Jane.

A low-slung sports car rolled close to their side of the street and stopped at the curb. A woman's voice called out the window, "Hi, wait a minute, kids."

Albert's mouth fell open. "Excellent," he said. They knew he meant the car.

A slight girl got out. Her froth of hair shone like polished silver. She was dressed in a plaid skirt, blue cardigan, knee socks, and loafers. Preppy, thought Philippa, immediately conscious of her own height and straight brown hair.

"May I accompany you to Clinton School," said the girl, "if that is where you are going?"

"Sure," said Jane. "Join the herd."

The girl bent to the car window. "These people are going to the school, so I am sure I will find the correct class." She blew a kiss. Philippa lowered her eyes in embarrassment at such an emotional display.

The car did a U-turn. Philippa caught a glimpse of spiky hair and a rolled-up sleeve. "Mother did not get up early enough to go with me to school as she had planned," said the girl.

Yah, never even got her hair combed, thought Philippa, and her hand strayed to the hidden knot in her own shoulder-length hair.

"Hi, I'm Jane. You can ignore these little kids. That's Laurie, and that's Philippa. You're new?"

"Yes, I have been staying with my father in Buffalo," said the girl, "till Mother found a house for us here. I am glad to meet you all. My name is Libby Barber." She smiled at the group. Her teeth were very white, as white as her hair; her eyes were deep blue, blue as a Siamese cat's.

"Excellent," breathed Albert. Philippa noticed the car had disappeared.

Jane tugged at Ted's hand, and they left Albert gawking behind them. "Perhaps you will direct me to the proper sixth grade," said Libby Barber. She offered Jane a slip of paper with a name and a number on it. Philippa wished this Buffalo girl did not talk so carefully.

"Miss Hurholtz, 6-A," Jane read. "That's our class."

Albert caught up with them and pressed the piece of yellow plastic into Libby's hand. He yodelled, "Yay-ay-ay-ay," as he rounded the corner of the school.

"What do you suppose this is?" said Libby. She extended the rectangle.

"I'll just take that," said Philippa. She snatched at the parking light. She did not want bits and pieces of her father's car passed to some stranger.

Surprisingly, Libby's fingers held firm. "That boy gave it to me. He must have had some reason, don't you think?"

"No, he didn't," said Philippa, "because he took it from our car, and he shouldn't have." She gave a jerk on the plastic, which cracked. Half of it came away in her hand.

"Of course, if it is yours," murmured Libby. She released the other half. Philippa thrust both jagged pieces deep in a back pocket.

"Ouch," Philippa said. She looked at the bloody scratch on her thumb.

"Oh, dear," said Libby. "You are hurt. You can wrap my handkerchief around it." She offered Philippa a white linen square with blue stitches decorating one corner.

"It's nothing," said Philippa. She sucked at the cut. She did not think anyone else her age owned a single hand-kerchief, especially not one with initials in blue embroidery.

2

Miss Hurholtz introduced Libby to the class. Libby batted her eyes in the direction of Albert, and he slid down in his chair until his chin rested on his desk.

"Please sit erect, Albert," said Miss Hurholtz. "I need everyone's attention. You remember I told you about our Columbus Day pageant. Today I have copies of the play this class is going to present." There were piles of dittoed sheets on her desk. Philippa left off frowning at Stupido Albert and gave all her attention to Miss Hurholtz. She loved to act.

"There is a character for everyone to play," said Miss Hurholtz. "We can have tryouts for the longest parts, and the class will vote, or I will assign parts alphabetically."

Laurie squeaked out, "Tryouts."

For as long as Philippa could remember, she and Jane had divided up the big parts in school plays. Everyone else was scared like Laurie or lazy like Albert. "Tryouts are fun," said Philippa.

Jane waved her hand. "Can girls try out for the men's parts?"

Albert hooted. Miss Hurholtz looked at him. Then she answered Jane, "I suppose you may, and vice versa, if any boys . . ." Groans drowned her out.

"Was there a role you had in mind, Jane?"

"Columbus," said Jane.

Philippa thought that was a smart idea. She and Jane would have a good time designing costumes for each other, because Philippa intended to play Queen Isabella.

Several boys tried out for Columbus. They were wooden compared to Jane. Everyone but Albert raised hands to vote for her.

Miss Hurholtz announced the part Philippa was waiting for. Philippa strode to the front of the room at Miss Hurholtz's nod and stool tall, majestic. She knew how to pace her reading so that the queen's prose rolled out across the classroom. Philippa spoke regally until she came to the line: "What better use for amethysts than searching wild western waters on behalf of holy saints." Something happened, and the words came out: "What besser ushe for ameshysts than shirtsing wild western wassers . . ."

She stopped. There were snorts of laughter. Philippa's chest heaved, but she must not laugh. To regain control she thought, My thumb hurts. She read the lines again with only a faint stutter at "western waters," and, composed, finished the rest of the speech. She sat down to applause.

Wow. That was hard.

"Libby, you're next," said Miss Hurholtz.

Philippa, catching her breath at her desk, sat up. New people seldom had the guts to try out for school plays.

Libby glided front, to the chair beside Miss Hurholtz's desk. She turned the chair to face the class, and then bowed to the left and to the right. She spread her skirt with a queer, slow gesture and sat down. Head high, she began to read from the script, which she held at arm's length. She did not hiss at those *S*'s and *H*'s. She spoke the words distinctly. Philippa was surprised how well her voice seemed to carry and how even the beat-up chair became a throne under Libby's skinny bottom.

At the end, Libby inserted two words of her own. "Advance, Columbus," she said, and rose with extended left hand.

Whatever got into Jane, Philippa did not know, but she marched right up the aisle. She grabbed Libby's hand. Jane knelt and pressed the hand to her forehead! Everyone clapped like crazy.

Libby, Libby Barber . . . *Libby was Isabella.*

Philippa was stunned. She had lost a tryout for the first time in her life.

Philippa merely existed, a machine, during the rest of the period. Her face felt stiff from keeping it pleasant.

She accepted one of the nonspeaking parts that no one had tried for, an Indian princess.

Inside, Philippa was shattered. She could not believe she had been cut out of this pageant by a newcomer. Well, not cut out, but with a measly part only good enough for some scaredy cat. Though stricken, Philippa was determined not to show her pain, ever.

When the class had math, Philippa allowed herself a glance at this Libby. Philippa stared at her clothes, her hair, her loafers, and at her bony wrists. She listened to that soft, icky voice explaining a problem.

The more Philippa stared at that silver-blond hair, the more she disliked it. The more she watched those thin hands holding chalk at the chalkboard, the more Philippa hated skinny fingers. Libby had an undernourished look. You could tell her grandmother did not feed her oatmeal. Libby made a miscalculation and smiled apologetically. She was an insipid, simpering nerd.

Libby returned to her desk, skirt swinging at her knees. She was dressed so carefully. Philippa smirked to herself. It was a mistake to wear clothes like that. Nobody else did.

Libby had probably made a mistake reading Isabella in such a slick way. She probably, really, did not know what she was doing. Like the math lesson—she had not known what she was doing there either.

Philippa decided this girl needed help, and she would be the one to help her. She could introduce her around, teach her about clothes and things like that.

At recess, Philippa approached Libby. "Hey," she said, "Jane and I always help each other with our costumes. My grandmother keeps a trunk of stuff we can use. We'll help with your robe, too."

Libby smiled at Philippa sweetly but shook her head. "No, thank you. My mother helps me." She turned away with a little flick of her pleats, as if she were still playing queen.

Jane came up in time to hear Libby's remark. "So let her mother help her. When can you and I go through that old trunk?"

"I'll ask," said Philippa. Abba's squirrellike habit of stashing away everything that might come in handy some-day was a plus, usually, for Philippa. Today it did not seem so fine.

It was the way Libby had said "my mother." It was . . . possessive. It reminded Philippa of a very old, babyish feeling of jealousy . . . of her own envy for girls who had real mothers at home to help them with clothes, or les-sons. Thinking of Libby, going home to "my mother" and getting an Isabella robe that hadn't first been a drape at a window, and a crown with jewels pasted on by a maternal hand, lipstick loaned, and eyeliner from her mother's bu-reau drawer—just thinking of it all gave Philippa's spit a sour taste.

At the cafeteria Philippa was very animated and talka-tive in the lunch line. She pretended not to see Libby in front of her. As Philippa riveted her attention on Jane at her left, she accidentally (ha-ha) bumped to the right against Libby's elbow. Jab. Libby's hand went *schmush* into her tomato soup. "Oh, I'm sorry," said Philippa. "Somebody must have pushed me." She rejoiced in the dismay in those Siamese cat's eyes.

"There's soup splattered on your sweater. Here's a napkin." And Philippa scrubbed at the tomato spots with a heavy hand, so the stains were rubbed in real well.

You could see Libby did not like to be dirty. Her lips sort of curled with distress. "Oh, don't," she said as Philippa continued rubbing. "It's all right." So polite! Philippa followed Libby to a table and sat beside her. As she ate enormous mouthfuls of hamburger, Philippa had to chew hard to keep from grinning.

Finally, as Libby's scrawny fingers strayed again and again to the smudges, Philippa said, "I guess your mother will have to help you get those out."

3

After school, Philippa didn't want to talk about the pageant. She told Jane and Laurie that she was going to stop by her father's office, and she ran for the bus.

Philippa liked to use the office copier to duplicate her best cartoons. In social studies she had created a new comic strip that she called "Bibby Larber." Seated alone in the rear of the bus, she looked at the series of cartoons, one by one: Bibby was shown wrapped in a plaid Roman toga in front of the class. She wore clogs with exaggerated high heels. The heels caught in the folds of the toga; Bibby stumbled, and her clogs flew off only to come down— bang—on Albert's head. Looking at the strip, Philippa felt better already.

When she got off the bus, she bought a package of gum at a corner newsstand. Blowing bubbles, Philippa entered the building where her father, an architect, had an office.

She went up the stairs to the second floor. A sign read: GEORGE CATLETT & ASSOCIATES. There was no one at the reception desk. Philippa slid open the door to the supply closet with a rasping squeak.

Someone bent over a drawing board in the corner jumped at the noise. A bottle of India ink fell to the floor. A blot spread. Philippa went to the washroom for paper towels.

"You startled me," complained the woman as she and Philippa mopped up the ink. "Did you want to see someone?"

On the floor, Philippa sucked at her gum. This was her territory. "I'm Philippa," Philippa said. Roy Jolliffe usually sat at that drawing board, and *he* usually rumpled Philippa's hair and said "Hi-kid."

"Philippa?" said the woman. As she brushed hair out of her eyes, the bracelets on her wrist clinked. The woman's hair, Philippa noticed, sort of spiked around her head in blond peaks. Philippa wondered was it real or permed to float out like that? This lady's clothes were nice. She wore a silky red striped shirt and navy harem trousers. In spite of a smudge on her nose, she looked like a model in a department store catalog—sophisticated and pretty.

"Philippa Catlett," said Philippa, answering the question in the woman's voice. "Is Dad in? Where's Roy and Mrs. Fargo?"

"Ohhhh," said the woman. "I didn't know. I'm Janet

Metz. I've just started to work here. Mrs. Fargo went to the bank. Roy and George are seeing a client."

"Moth-err!" A too-familiar voice drifted up the stairs, and a head so blond it was white appeared through the railings.

The woman turned. "Hi, sweetie! How was the first day at the new school?"

Libby threw her arms (with soup stains on one sleeve) around the woman. "Mother! I am going to be in a school pageant. Isn't that wonderful?"

"Splendid," said the woman. "Libby, dear, do you know Philippa?"

"We're in the same class," said Philippa.

"Yes," said Libby. "I didn't know your mother worked here, too."

Chewing gum rapidly, Philippa said, "This is my father's office." What a nerd. Everybody knew Philippa lived with her father and her grandparents, and that Philippa's mother had died a long, long time ago.

"And now it is my mother's as well," said Libby, smiling.

Philippa stared until Libby's face sobered. Philippa returned to the supply closet.

"Is there something I can get for you?" said Libby's mother, as if she'd been left like a guard dog or something. Philippa was glad to hear the door below open. She ran to the railing.

"Hi-kid," said Roy.

" 'Lo, Flip," said her father. "Didn't expect to find you here." He took the stairs two at a time, and Philippa noticed, as he put an arm around her for one of his big, welcoming hugs, he said hi to Libby. So he'd met her already!

"Guess you've met Libby and our newest associate, Miss Metz," said Philippa's father.

"My mother, Mrs. Barber," said Libby.

"Yeah," said Philippa's father, "our associate Janet Metz-Barber. Hyphens are hard to remember around an office."

"You know I only use 'Janet Metz' at work, dear," said the woman. "I'm always Mrs. Barber at home." Libby subsided on the waiting-room couch with a book.

Philippa made three copies of her comic strip on the copying machine. Maybe she'd send it to *MAD* magazine. Suddenly both girls were startled by a little moan from Libby's mother, "Uh-oo! I just finished these!"

"I know," said Philippa's father, "but the customer is paying for the changes, so it's up to us to do them fresh."

Miss Metz sighed. "If you give me a key, I'll come back tonight and redo the whole set."

Roy said, "You can have my key. All right, George?"

In her father's one-headlighted car, on the way home, Philippa asked about the Metz-Barbers. "She's a friend of Roy's," her father said. "We have to work under pressure sometimes. I'm not sure she's up to it."

They drove in silence for a moment. Philippa said, "That Libby is in my class."

"Mmhm."

"She thinks she is good at acting."

Philippa's father shifted at a yield sign. "That's nice. Gives you something in common."

"Yeah. Well. Her mother looks like a witch with that fuzzy hair all over the place."

Her father laughed. "So long as she works hard, I don't care if she's a witch."

"Witches cast spells," said Philippa, but her father only patted her knee.

4

A few days later Jane and Philippa sat on Abba's garden fence. An old brick school, unused and desolate, loomed behind them. Abba often said, "That place ought to have been torn down long ago. Don't put a foot on those fire escapes. They're dangerous."

Of course, Jane and Philippa had been on both fire escapes at least twice. They climbed the school fence so often, its chain links sagged back and forth. Abba's fence, lower and sturdier, had a plank across the top where Jane and Philippa sat to lick the centers from chocolate cream-filled cookies.

Jane said, "I don't have to baby-sit today. Do you think your grandmother'd let us hunt for costumes in the attic?"

"Let's find out," said Philippa. As they entered the kitchen, Jack wagged his tail, but Abba frowned. Philippa knew Abba was thinking that Jane did not take enough baths.

"Yes, but wash your hands first," said Abba in answer to the girls' request.

"Why?" said Philippa. "We'll only get dusty in the attic."

"I don't want fingerprints on the walls," said Abba.

Going up the stairs to the third floor, Philippa drummed on the wall. Not a print appeared, but Jane got excited. "Listen, Phil, we got to have a drum with your Indian costume. You can play it when you're introduced at Isabella's court."

"And dance!" said Philippa. "How about that?" She opened the door to the attic. It was piled with cartons, silver hatboxes, chairs with sat-through seats. Philippa did a hopping dance around a large trunk.

"Phil, you do that, and everybody'll look at you, instead of Queen Libby."

Philippa halted, hands on hips. "You sure were no help at the tryouts. Kneeling at her feet!" Philippa heaved the trunk open and scowled into a top drawer.

"Mm, I know. It was a real bummer. Her act was so good, though, it was like I got carried away with it. Dancing would be super the same way. You'd steal the show."

"There isn't a dance written in the script."

"It isn't written *out*, either. Miss Hurholtz likes us to show our creative imaginations. Here—" Jane emptied one of the hatboxes. She hung it by its braided cord around Philippa's neck. Philippa began to thump on the cardboard. Her knees bent and her feet *kathumped* the floor, *bbbbonk, bbbbonk.*

"Faster," said Jane.

There was a war whoop from Abba on the floor below. "Phil-lip-puh! You will put a hole in the ceiling. Your father wants you. Come down this instant."

"Oops," said Jane. "I better go."

Jane took an old velvet curtain and a hat with a curling feather and went home. Philippa asked Abba, "Why is Dad home so early?"

"He's borrowed a car to do some shopping," said Abba, "while he gets that fender fixed." Philippa and her father often went grocery shopping for Abba, but usually on Saturdays; then they had double-dip chocolate ice cream cones afterward. Philippa zipped up her jacket and ran outside.

Her father stood by the open door of a green sports car. It looked familiar. "There's room in back," he said. He pulled the bucket seat forward. Philippa squeezed into the back and almost fell onto Libby as her father impatiently righted the seat. Behind the steering wheel was Libby's mother. Her father had not only borrowed a car; he'd borrowed a driver!

"We could use Abba's car," said Philippa.

"It's slow as a turtle," said her father. "Your friend Libby heard about a new store. Janet offered to take us." The car rolled forward with a throaty roar.

Philippa wanted to yell that she and Libby were not friends. To cover her hostility, she fumbled the bag of cookies from her pocket and held it toward the front seat.

Her father took one and offered it to the driver. "Have a bite, Miss Metz?"

"Mrs. Barber," said Libby. "Mother is out of the office now."

"Of course, sweetie," said Libby's mother. "Metz is only my working name. But don't worry—I'm always Mrs. Barber, too."

"Right. We'll remember that, okay, Flip?" said Philippa's father.

"Sure," said Philippa with little interest. She thought it was Libby's problem anyway.

Her father offered the bag to Libby before returning it to Philippa. "No, thank you," said Libby. "Chocolate is bad for my complexion."

Philippa crammed a whole cookie into her mouth, and then another. She choked. Libby patted her between the shoulders.

When Philippa wiped the coughing tears from her eyes, she realized the train tracks were not far away. In this part of town, the buildings were tacky, rundown. Her voice still gravelly from chocolate crumbs, Philippa croaked, "Dad, where are we going?"

Her father was so busy talking and laughing with Libby's mother, he did not hear her. With or without hyphens, Libby's mother must have worked out fine at the office, he seemed so pleased with her. Feeling nobody cared, Philippa did not repeat her question.

Libby said, "We're going to Jolly Joan's."

"I never heard of that supermarket."

"It's not a supermarket. It's a health food store."

Mrs. Barber turned the car into an empty lot. When Philippa crawled out, her sneakers crunched on pulverized bricks. In a corner of the parking lot stood a bulldozer. A crane hung over the rooftops. It seemed to Philippa that everything that wasn't already falling down was being torn down. The surrounding emptiness bothered her, but all she said was, "Isn't this a dumpy place to have a store?"

"Part of the area is going into condominiums," said her father. "We're thinking of buying one of the brownstones and relocating our office. We need more space."

"In this crappy place?" said Philippa.

Mrs. Barber laughed. Her hair seemed spikier than ever, her blue eyes seemed bluer, and her smile offered instant charm. She seemed very—alive. "It would be such a challenge to fix over," she said. Philippa's father put his hand under Mrs. Barber's arm as if to help guide her high-heeled boots over the bricks. Mrs. Barber was short for her father to walk with. He had to bend his head to speak in her ear, in a superfriendly sort of way. Philippa crossed the lot after them, Libby beside her. They entered a double door under a hand-lettered sign: JOLLY JOAN.

Inside, Philippa saw that the store was narrow but deep. Green plants hung under the fluorescent lights, with skeins of red onions and garlic between them. Suddenly, her nose tickled. "Something's burning," Philippa said.

"Sandalwood," said Libby. "Jolly Joan sells incense. I love it."

Philippa suddenly was caught in a paroxysm of sneezes. This store smelled gross and looked dusty and down-at-the-heels. It was definitely not the kind of place where Abba, who liked everything spotless, would buy anything.

Where was her father? Philippa wanted his company in this creepy store. She found him under a shedlike extension. Mrs. Barber was with him. They were looking at orange globes labeled PERSIMMONS. "Oranges don't cost that much at the Lucky Market," Philippa said, feeling like her grandmother.

"These are organically grown," said Mrs. Barber. Philippa thought of the liver and kidney diagrams in her science book; they were organs. She did not want to know how they grew.

The sign across from her was better: HONEY. But wait, FROM PREHISTORIC BEES, it said. Was she supposed to believe this honey came from the Age of the Dinosaurs? She wanted her father to read it. He'd say something like, "There's a sucker born every minute, Flip," but he was so interested in Mrs. Barber's grocery list and in helping her hold it that he did not even see Philippa beckoning to him.

Philippa wandered to the front of the store. She met Libby, who watched a bearded man weigh out grain from a large sack. "I find bulghur wheat delicious," Libby said, "don't you?"

"I never had any," said Philippa. She was ready to go home.

But it was a while longer before her father said, "Come on, Flip. It's late." He gave her a bag to carry; the tops of carrots swayed out from it like green flags.

Three boxes and Philippa's bag went into the backseat between her and Libby. "I don't know where you'll put the meat when we get it," said Philippa. "Where is the health meat store?"

Libby put her hand to her forehead and leaned into her corner. She shuddered. "Meat!" It was only a whisper.

Mrs. Barber said, "This season Libby is vegetarian."

Vegetables were Philippa's least interesting foods. "Does that mean you never eat a hamburger?"

"Gro-ossss," said Libby.

Philippa said, "I love hamburgers with lots of ketchup."

Libby flickered those Siamese cat's eyes over Philippa. "Fish is delightful," she announced.

"Fish stinks," said Philippa.

"Not when it is fresh," said Libby.

"I mean, I don't like it," said Philippa.

Her father interrupted. "Well, you don't have to eat it!"

Philippa was surprised at how tart he sounded. Her feelings were hurt.

Mrs. Barber let Philippa and her father off in front of the gashed maple. Mr. Catlett stood and said good-bye in the autumn twilight. Philippa had had her fill of Libby and her mother. She dashed into the house.

When Philippa's father elbowed the kitchen door open and placed his bag of groceries on the table, Abba poked into it. She lifted out a plastic container. "Tofu—bean curd. I do not believe I know how to cook this, George."

Her father brought out a swollen-looking vegetable with stems and leaves ten inches long. "I bought a bok choy—for a change. If you need a recipe, Ma, I'll get one from Janet. She cooks it, and it tastes fine."

He'd already eaten at the Barbers' then. Philippa asked, "What does Mr. Barber eat?"

"Doesn't live here," said her father. "They're divorced." Philippa remembered that Libby had stayed with her father in Buffalo.

Abba was unsettled by the groceries. "If you don't fill a man's stomach with good red meat once in a while, divorce is what you can expect."

Philippa's father hit the table with the bok choy. "See here, Ma, it doesn't do to be so damned old-fashioned. Vegetables are good for you. They keep you thin." He had Abba there.

Abba was used to having the last word. She said, "Families that eat together, live together." Philippa's father laughed. Pop tried to say something, which made Jack bark, and it got so noisy that Philippa had to yell to make herself heard.

"How about we eat the bean curd with chocolate sauce?"

Her father cocked an eyebrow at her. "Don't know, but you can call your friend, Libby, and ask her."

"She's not my friend," said Philippa, "and chocolate is bad for her complexion." Philippa flounced up to her room and flung herself on her bed, facedown.

People who kept shoving other people down your throat to be your friends were mean and inconsiderate. This had been one TS of a day. Without Abba around, she muttered "Tough shitty shit" into her pillow.

5

On Wednesday, Abba interrupted Philippa's homework. "Invite Libby Barber to stay overnight Friday.
Telephone and invite her properly."

Abba would not let Philippa invite Jane for a sleepover, and Jane was her best friend. "NO!" hollered Philippa.

At dinner that evening, Philippa's father said, "Flip,
it was my idea that Libby spend Friday night here. Her
mother and I are going to the theater in the city."

Philippa did not look at him. She said, "I thought you
said Libby's mother was Roy's friend."

"Yes, and Roy and his wife are going with us. Janet
could get a baby-sitter, but it's nicer for Libby to stay
here."

How could her father be so blind to how people got
along together? He went right on. "You have to remember Libby's been alone a lot, with her mother working.

She's been signed into community centers after school, putting on plays and taking ballet. She'll enjoy being here with you."

Putting on plays. Uh huh. That's how she'd pulled the Isabella part out from under Philippa's nose. Philippa did not feel one bit sorry for Libby.

Her father was coaxing. "How about it, hm?"

He'd go right on asking, time after time, if Philippa did not take matters into her own hands. Maybe what she should do was, well, give Libby such a jolt that she would never again accept a Catlett invitation.

Philippa kept her eyes on her plate. "She can come," she said. She'd figure something out.

Mrs. Barber dropped Libby off Friday afternoon. Abba went to the door. "Come in, dear. What a pretty coat. And new boots? Stunning. Philippa? Where are you?"

Philippa was upstairs. She had dragged a folding cot down from the attic and unrolled her sleeping bag on it. Abba had made her remove the Bibby Larber comic strips from her bulletin board.

Philippa had decided to take Libby to Jane's street, where she could count on finding a good rowdy street game. Libby did not seem like a street-game player.

Philippa went downstairs. Libby had unbuttoned her coat. "Leave it on," said Philippa. "We're going out."

"See here," said Abba, "find a place for Libby to unpack."

"My room is upstairs and to the left," said Philippa, but Abba pressed her lips together and looked daggers.

"Oh, you mean show her," said Philippa to Abba, and then to Libby, "Bring your stuff." A blue overnight case lay on Pop's footstool. Not a fingerprint marred the brass fittings. The last time Philippa had stayed overnight at Laurie's, she'd taken her pajamas and toothbrush in a brown paper bag. Like the embroidered handkerchief, this had initials, too, ERB. E for Elizabeth; she wondered what the R stood for. *Repulsive,* offered an inner voice.

Libby picked up the blue case and followed Philippa. "I love sleeping over. It is so nice to have your invitation."

"Sure," said Philippa, thinking, If you only knew how Dad put the pressure on.

"Oh, what a marvelous quilt. Your grandmother has the most interesting antiques." Knock it off, thought Philippa.

Libby snapped open the blue case. She took out a frilled gown and placed it on the head of the bed. "That's where *I* sleep," burst out of Philippa. "Uh, usually, that is. I get the sleeping bag tonight."

Libby gathered the gown to her sweater front. "I don't mind sleeping on the cot," she said. "Sleeping bags are fun."

Abba would never allow that. "Forget it," Philippa said. "You're the guest. Unpack so we can go outside."

Philippa was downstairs before Libby finished. "Abba,"

33

she said, "I think I ought to show Libby where everything is in the neighborhood."

"Yes," said Abba, "and I need you to shop for me. I need bread from the bakery at Hamilton and Market."

Perfect, thought Philippa.

Abba smiled as Libby came downstairs. "I understand you like vegetables and grains, dear. Buy a dozen whole wheat rolls and a loaf of protein bread."

Philippa stared at Abba. "What's for dinner?" she asked.

"Pea soup," said Abba, "since Libby likes vegetables."

All right! Abba made pea soup from scratch, and it tasted so good it was weird to think it was vegetables.

Philippa rushed them to the bakery and out again so fast she forgot the change. Libby ran back for it and caught up with Philippa at the head of Putney Street. Jane's street had a lived-in look that Philippa appreciated, even though Abba did not. Libby wrinkled her nose at the first driveway. A dog had torn open a sack of trash and strewn smeary papers. Libby tiptoed in her new boots around each sticky heap.

When they approached the old school, she said, "That building is so gloomy, isn't it?"

"Nowhere's near so gloomy as Jolly Joan's," said Philippa. "That school's been there all my life. Dad went there when he was my age."

"Heads up!" came a shout. A football spun in front of Libby and bounced on the sidewalk. Libby shrank away.

As if it would explode, Philippa thought. A large boy in a gray sweatshirt ran out of the school yard and scooped up the ball.

"People are not careful here," Libby observed.

"There's Jane," said Philippa, and she ran. Libby, who had had enough running to retrieve change from the bakery, dropped behind. Philippa pushed into the crowd of Jane and younger children. Everybody shoved at a huge carton. It said, GE RANGE.

"Hi, Phil," said Jane. To the rest she shouted, "Heave." The carton turned over, *plonk*, and a muffled "wow" came from inside.

Jane looked past Philippa. "I see Libby really came, the way you said."

Philippa grunted a little, then asked, "Who's inside?"

When the box was pushed upright, Denise poked her head out. She brushed hair from her eyes. "That's so great," Denise said. "It's a tumble box. Jane invented it."

"Want to try, Phil?"

"Sure." Philippa lowered herself into the carton as Libby joined them.

Without greeting anyone, Libby walked over to the box and said, "Philippa, what are you going to do in there? Your grandmother expects us." Philippa could tell Libby was upset, because she did not even say a polite hi to Jane.

"We got plenty of time." Philippa hunkered deep inside. Someone yanked the flaps together over her head, and the box began to teeter.

"Hold your head," yelled Jane. "You got to hold your head so it doesn't smack when you go upside down." Over Philippa went, and her doubled-up knees gave her chin a smart rap. Bottoms up, Philippa had a moment of insight. This was exactly the kind of fun Libby would hate.

"Over again?" shouted Jane.

Philippa somersaulted and popped up. "No, but it's really super. Makes you dizzy. Try it, Lib."

Libby stroked her coat buttons. "No, thanks."

"Party-pooper," said Philippa. She got out of the box and leaned against a light post. If she could just get Miss Superclean inside.

Herbert Overracker did what Philippa could not do. Herbert was the youngest of the family and went to a day care center. He unwound himself from a red tricycle and shuffled toward Libby. When he slipped a very dirty hand into Libby's, Libby said, "Oh!" looked down, and actually smiled into Herbert's brown eyes. Her hand, Philippa saw with amazement, tightened around Herbert's.

"Where did you come from?" said Libby.

"It's only Herbert," said Jane. "He's been in a snit the whole afternoon."

Herbert's face was marked with dry tear streaks, and his nose ran. He wore a tweed cap snapped under his chin and a tweed jacket with a brown velvet collar to match his eyes. The cap and jacket had come from the Next-to-New Shop. They gave him a certain British dash. Herbert blinked his extra long lashes at Libby. "What's your name?" he said softly.

"My name is Libby," said Libby. "Elizabeth Ruth Barber. How old are you, Herbert?"

"Four, I think. I want to go in the box with you."

"Huh!" said Jane. "He wouldn't go with me or Denise or Amber or by himself. He's too scared."

"I'm not scared of her—going with her," said Herbert. He coughed a gentle rattle, and his eyes, rolled up at Libby under the visor of the cap, were brown pools of love. They were putting Libby on the spot.

"Maybe next time," said Libby. She tried to drop Herbert's grimy hand. His fingers were twined tightly into hers.

"I want to go with you," said Herbert. His eyes filled with tears.

"Please don't cry," Libby said. Philippa could tell that Libby was not used to little kids. Libby did not know that Herbert liked strangers better than his family. He'd once spent a whole Saturday cadging candy from strangers at a supermarket while Jane searched for him.

Libby walked to the tumble box with Herbert. "Once," she said. "Can you show me how to do it? Do you sit in my lap?"

Libby had to squat in the box and hold Herbert between the skirts of her full coat. "We'll push real easy," Jane said, "so he doesn't whack too bad."

Once was not enough for Herbert. They tumbled three times. Herbert giggled and giggled. There was not even an "oh!" from Libby.

When Libby climbed out of the box after Herbert, Philippa rejoiced to see that her blond hair was scraggly. She saw Libby glance at the wrinkles in her coat where Herbert had sat. Libby smiled at Herbert, though, when they said good-bye.

In case Libby had not noticed, "I think you got finger-prints on your coat," said Philippa. She steered Libby into the school yard.

"Oh, dear. He wasn't very clean. But so sweet. I'll tell Mother about that neglected little child, and she'll under-stand," Libby said.

Together they walked over the old flagstones and be-yond the rear fire escape. "See," said Philippa, "that's our house over there." She gestured toward the tall white house that showed through the trees.

"But there is a terrible fence in the way," said Libby. "Why are we coming here?"

"It's a shortcut," said Philippa. "You don't want to run around the block now it's so late, do you?"

"It wouldn't be so late if you hadn't played at Jane's."

"You'd have missed that sweet little Herbert," said Philippa.

For a minute there was silence. Then Libby said, "All right, Philippa. You think I'm silly sometimes, don't you?"

"You said it, not me," breathed Philippa. Louder, she said, "Here's the fence."

It was really two fences. The school's chain link fence met the lower Catlett fence at right angles. Philippa said, "All you have to do is get over the big one and drop down onto our fence. Watch me. It's easy." Philippa tossed the bag of bread over the fence into the Catletts' garden.

Scrambling up swiftly, she let herself swing backwards, swaying with the chain links. At the top, her weight swung her forward. Then she stepped down onto the top board of the Catletts' fence. From there she hopped down to the ground. She turned to see what Libby would do.

Slowly, Libby inserted one shiny boot in the wire mesh, then the other. The links went backwards. "Eeeee," went Libby.

"Don't worry. When you get higher, you'll lean this way," said Philippa.

Libby pushed her left toe into a higher link and struggled upward. As she reached the top and got one leg over the sharp, pointed ends, the fence swung her forward. "Ooooo," went Libby. Better and better!

The wire, as Libby stepped over, goudged the instep of one boot. The hem of her coat caught on a barb and ripped. Trying to free it, Libby was practically bent into a pretzel. Philippa pretended her laugh was a cough.

With her coat free, Libby lowered herself carefully to the top board of the Catlett fence, then hesitated. "What do I do now?" she said as she crouched there.

Philippa could barely get the word out for helpless laughter. "J-jump," she said. It was only three feet, so why not?

Libby jumped. She landed with one boot heel caught in the frazzled hem. Pulled sidewise, Libby fell flat. Her coat fell apart and her skirt flew up.

Philippa went hot and strange. She felt like a skunk. An enemy down and out was so defenseless, it was no fun.

Libby was up immediately, brushing off twigs and dirt. She strained to see over her shoulder. "Is there mud on my back, Philippa?"

To keep her disturbing thoughts away, Philippa said, "You ought not to step on your coat." She swept her hand over the wool vigorously, then marched straight ahead to the kitchen door.

Once there, she turned to Libby. "I wouldn't mention we came by Jane's if I were you."

Libby's blue eyes bored deeply into Philippa's gray ones. "I know. You think I'm going to tell your grandmother about that fence and everything, don't you?"

Philippa muttered, "Who cares?" and pushed hurriedly into the kitchen.

Inside, they were overwhelmed with the aroma of pea soup. Abba stood over a strainer and pressed a blob of cooked peas through it with a wooden spoon. "It's about time you showed up," Abba said. "Where did Philippa take you, dear?"

Libby sank onto a stool and sighed. "To many interesting places, Mrs. Catlett. It's *so* nice to be here where it smells wonderful."

Abba smiled. "And nice to have you. One of you set the big table, please?"

Libby rose immediately. "I love to help," she said. "I'll hang up my coat." She disappeared toward the hall closet.

"Give that bone to Jack," said Abba to Philippa. "Put it on a newspaper out of the way."

Philippa felt the hambone, which had stewed with the peas, to see if it was cool. Then she bent down to smile at the dog under the kitchen table. He drizzled a strand of saliva from one side of his gray muzzle, and his soulful eyes gazed toward the bone.

Libby returned. She had combed her hair and looked neat without the soiled coat. "Mrs. Catlett, where do you keep the silver? In the dining room?"

"There. In the drawer." Abba motioned with her spoon.

Libby stepped to the table. There was a rush of claws and a snapping of long yellow teeth. "Grrr-wow-wowowowowff," erupted at her ankles.

"Eeeeekk," squealed Libby and jumped a foot. Knives and forks clattered to the floor.

"Jack! Behave yourself!" said Abba, and crossly to Philippa, "I told you to put him out of the way. He goes wild over bones."

"He scares me," Libby said. "Would you pick those up for me, Philippa, please?"

Philippa knelt and patted Jack before gathering up the

fallen silver. "Good boy," she whispered. Jack rumbled in his throat. Jack knew an enemy from a friend!

When Abba had tied a large napkin under Pop's chin, so he would not spill soup in case his hand trembled, she ladled full plates from the rosebud tureen. Philippa buttered her roll and slurped with her soup spoon, she was so hungry.

But Libby! She was fishing out every shred of ham that floated in the soup. Abba said, "My stars, child, I didn't realize how thorough a vegetarian you are. Would you like scrambled eggs?"

"Oh, no, thank you," said Libby. "This is so delicious. Peas are quite nourishing, you know." Libby sipped from her spoon dreamily. "It is so relaxing to be here, while my mother spends time with someone she admires."

Philippa spluttered. She had to wipe her chin. It was stupid, the way Libby phrased ordinary things like people eating together. Libby continued. "It must be romantic to have a candlelight dinner." Philippa wished she could forget that Libby had not told Abba about the fence.

Disturbed, she observed, "You can't eat candlelight."

Libby gave a knowing little laugh. "You're right. Eating is not important when you are enjoying yourself in other ways."

"What other ways?"

Libby removed another crumb of meat. "Sometimes, people have stars in their eyes. That's what people say, you know."

"What people?"

Libby didn't answer. Instead she smiled into her soup.

Abba went to the kitchen for more hot bread. As if Pop were a dummy and could not hear, Libby whispered loudly to Philippa, "Mutual attraction means nothing else is important."

Philippa's roll did not seem as fresh as she thought it should be. As she put it aside, she thought of everything Libby had been through that day: Jack had frightened her; Abba had added meat to the soup; and she herself had put Libby through an ordeal by mud and fence. None of it mattered. Libby's face glowed with romantic thoughts of her mother and Philippa's father somewhere, together. Libby was a problem, but not *the* problem. *The* problem was her mother. How dare Philippa's father get involved with some spiky-haired female that was Libby Barber's mother?

Philippa's fingers twitched. She needed a clean sheet of paper and her drawing pencil. She would draw a witch riding a drawing board and brandishing an architect's T-square instead of a broom. Yes. And make Libby a cat clinging to the witch's cape.

Pushing her chair back, Philippa said, "I don't want dessert. May I please be excused?"

6

Philippa was reluctant to approach Miss Hurholtz about playing the part of a dancing Indian princess. At the end of class, the following week, Jane forced Philippa to stop at Miss Hurholtz's desk and ask.

"About my Indian princess part in the pageant?" said Philippa. "I have a, an addition——"

"Some stage business," said Jane beside her.

Miss Hurholtz narrowed her eyes at Philippa. Philippa fidgeted. Maybe the dance was not such a great idea, she thought. Miss Hurholtz sighed. Then Philippa knew it was not a good idea. Miss Hurholtz said, "We have lost a major performer."

Jane asked, "Who did we lose?"

"Whom, Jane. We lost Libby. Libby is sick, and her mother isn't sure she will be well in time."

Jane said, "That's too bad. What's she got? Is it chicken pox?"

"That's exactly what she has. Seems a funny time of year for it. How did you know?"

"My little brother has it."

"Herbert!" exclaimed Philippa.

"I did not realize Libby knew your family, Jane."

"Well," Jane said, "she was playing with my brother the afternoon he was coming down with chicken pox. Only, we didn't know it till he broke out with bumps at suppertime."

Philippa thought maybe she'd take Herbert some bubble gum the next time she saw him.

Miss Hurholtz said to Jane, "Will you take Libby's books and assignments to her?"

Jane shook her head. "I have to baby-sit."

"Philippa, how about you?" asked Miss Hurholtz.

Philippa was imagining how people in olden times, like Queen Isabella's, were always dying of plagues. Miss Hurholtz repeated, "Philippa?"

Philippa stopped smiling. "M-me? No, I can't. Uh, my grandmother needs me."

Jane said, "You got time. You can see how sick Libby is."

Philippa did not care how sick Libby was—the sicker the better—but she knew Jane was telling her something.

Jane went on, "If you find out how long she's going to be sick, then Miss Hurholtz knows whether someone else has to learn her part."

"Poor Libby," said Miss Hurholtz. "Here she is just getting used to a new school. Don't go inside, Philippa, if you have not had chicken pox."

"I had it," said Philippa. She remembered Abba giving her baths of bicarbonate of soda for the intolerable itch. She hoped Libby was itching all over.

Outside room 6-A, Jane hissed to Philippa, "If somebody else has to play the queen, it'll be you. Ask about Libby's costume, okay? Libby's ma won't want to waste it."

Philippa said, "But my dress is done. The fringe looks terrific." Philippa was not sure she wanted to wear any garment intended for Bibby Larber.

"Maybe Libby will get well. Then you dance. If she doesn't, then you're ready. You got to be prepared—that's long-range planning, Phil." Jane walked beside Philippa toward the exit where Laurie always waited to walk home with them. Amber, Denise, and Ted sat on the wall outside.

"C'mon kids," said Jane. "No stalling now. Remember, Phil, long-range planning." She hustled the kids up the block.

"What's that mean?" said Laurie.

"Uh," said Philippa, "I have to take these books to Libby's house. You want to walk there with me?"

They scuffed through fallen leaves for several blocks, crossed a little park with two benches, and entered Sycamore Lane.

At number 22, Philippa lifted a brass knocker. An older woman, Libby's grandmother probably, opened the door. "Hello, girls. I'm Mrs. Bigelow. If you've had chicken pox, you can come in. Elizabeth needs a bit of company."

"I don't think I've had it," said Laurie. "I'll wait out here." She sat on a railing of the tiny porch. Philippa went in.

The grandmother closed the door behind Philippa. With the two of them in the hall, the space was completely used up. Philippa saw a flight of stairs straight ahead, while an arch led right and another door left. "Elizabeth is in the living room," Mrs. Bigelow said.

Philippa went through the arch. She saw a fireplace. There were hot coals in it, the remains of a fire. To her left was a three-sided alcove of windows flooded with afternoon sunshine. The alcove held a table and four chairs. Had Philippa's father eaten the bok choy there?

There were no antiques, as at Abba and Pop's. Everything was plain, but full of colors. A poster over the fireplace was nothing but slashes of red and purple. The television set, volume tuned low, flickered on a lime-green shelf.

"I'm over here." Philippa turned to a brown-and-white flowered couch. Libby lay there wrapped in a satin quilt. Her face was lumpy with pox and as pink as the quilt.

"I brought your homework." Philippa placed the books and papers on the coffee table. She did not know how to introduce the subject of Isabella. The moment throbbed with silence.

Then, "Eee-ooo, Philippa!" exclaimed Libby. "Don't stare at me like that. I know I am a terrible sight." She sank into the quilt till only her blond hair showed.

Philippa wished Jane had come. Jane knew how to get to the heart of the matter. Philippa turned to escape, but the grandmother blocked the way with a bowl of whole wheat crackers and a glass pitcher of orange juice. "Have a snack with Elizabeth. I'll take a plate to the little girl outside."

"Who's outside?" said Libby as she emerged from the quilt.

"Laurie," said Philippa. "She hasn't had chicken pox. Do you know, uh, how long it lasts?"

"Forever!" wailed Libby.

"T-t-ttt," said Mrs. Bigelow. She plumped up Libby's pillow and urged a glass into Libby's hand. "I've seen cases last three days. Of course, the older you are, the longer you have it. It could take two weeks, I suppose."

"The Columbus Day pageant is next Friday," Philippa said casually.

"I know. I can't possibly make a public appearance then. Philippa, you will have to learn my part in a hurry."

Libby groaned. Philippa eyed her. "Why me?" she asked. But she knew why her. She wanted it.

Libby swallowed a tiny mouthful of orange juice. "Mother has my robe and a long dress cut out and basted together. She can fit it to you instead of me."

Philippa ate seven whole-wheat crackers to fill her fluttery stomach.

Later, walking home in the October twilight, Laurie said, "How long is Libby going to be sick?"

Philippa leaped from sidewalk crack to sidewalk crack. Having caught a dozen cracks with her Pumas, she answered. "Anywhere from three days to two weeks."

"If it's two weeks, you'll get to be Isabella, won't you?"

"Wellll, I can get prepared. That's long-range planning, you know. But really, it depends." Philippa practiced a broad jump as if she had springs on her feet.

"Depends on what?"

"I have to think about it, don't I?" Philippa hollered over her shoulder. "It depends on whether I want to, that's what."

7

Miss Hurholtz said the pageant needed Philippa, so Philippa went into intensive training. She practiced reciting to Laurie and the Overrackers on the way to school, and to Abba and Pop at breakfast and dinner. "Watch you don't spill that milk," said Abba, "waving your arms like that."

"You got Libby's costume yet?" said Jane.

Philippa wanted that costume—and yet, she didn't. "If you help me, we can get a dress out of something in Abba's trunk."

Jane said, "When you're on the stage, you have to do what's best for the show. Telephone Libby this afternoon."

Philippa had to dial the Barbers' number twice. She got a wrong number when her finger slipped the first time. At the second try, Libby answered. "Mother said you and your father can come for dinner, and she'll fit the costume to you. Tonight's all right."

Dazed that Libby was so open-handed, Philippa said to Abba, "Dad and I are invited to the Barbers for dinner. I don't have to go if you don't want me to."

"By all means go," said Abba, "but you'd better ask your father if he is free."

Philippa dialed again. "George Catlett and Associates," a woman's voice, not Mrs. Fargo's, answered. "Janet Metz speaking."

Philippa hesitated. She did not remember who Janet Metz was. Then it occurred to her that that was Mrs. Barber's working name. "Yes?" said Mrs. Metz-Barber, "may I help you?"

"This is Philippa," said Philippa. "Can I talk to my father?"

"How are you, Philippa? I'll take a message. He's in a meeting right now."

"Well, it's about that Columbus Day dress," said Philippa. "Libby says it can fit me, and I'm to see if Dad can come."

Mrs. Barber was cordial. "Yes, the robe's done. I can fit the dress to you easily. I mentioned dinner to your father. Come at six-thirty?"

"All right," said Philippa. Abba reminded Philippa that she forgot to say thank you when she hung up.

A little nervous, Philippa appeared at 22 Sycamore Lane at six thirty-five. She was going to be alone with Mrs. Barber and Libby because, after all, her father could not come till it was time to go home. Mrs. Barber, wearing a short apron over black corduroy knickers, opened the door.

"This is so nice. It gives me a chance to know you better, Philippa." They went into the living room.

There was Libby. She wore a blue housecoat. Scabs dotted her forehead. She was lighting the candles on the dining room table. "We're having candles tonight so my chicken pox won't look so awful. I love candlelight." Philippa knew that already. She was more concerned about what vegetarians ate.

When Mrs. Barber carried in a casserole, Philippa was relieved that the smells were not too bad. While Libby ate bits of this and that, Philippa finished everything. She had never had a meal like this at Abba's. The casserole contained brown rice, with shrimp and mushrooms cooked in it. There was a green salad with avocados and grapefruit. Philippa gobbled a second helping of both, but ate around the grapefruit the second time. She filled in the empty spaces with pumpkin bread.

"You're not eating very much, Libby," said Mrs. Barber. "I made one of your favorite dinners."

"Thank you," said Libby, "but I am not very hungry."

Mrs. Barber stroked Libby's cheek. "I'll warm a glass of milk at bedtime," she said. Libby smiled gratefully. Philippa wondered how anyone could stand warm milk.

After dinner, Libby returned to the sofa with a sigh of weariness. "Now," said Mrs. Barber to Philippa, "you must try on the outfit. I left it in Libby's room. Put it on so I can fit it properly."

In Libby's room, Philippa gazed around curiously. There

were tiers of shelves, painted pink on the inside, to show off a collection of coral, shells, and a dried starfish. There were books, lots of them. There were stacks of colored paper, boxes of crayons, paints and magic markers, nice and neat, not stuck into jelly jars the way Philippa kept hers. Over the bed was a black-and-silver poster of a horse pawing the air with its silver hooves. A handwritten title was tacked underneath: TO CHASE AWAY NIGHTMARES. Philippa stared at it. Nobody ever gave her a poster to chase away scary dreams.

The dress was on the bed. Philippa inched into it carefully because Libby's mother had opened a seam. Philippa was wider than Libby. Anybody with normal eating habits would be wider than Libby. Philippa held the dress together with one hand and looked at herself in the long mirror. Not bad, not bad at all! On second thought, why quibble. She looked terrific. The dress was red, with glinty threads in it. It fell across Philippa's upper arms in a graceful fold.

Instead of purple, which Philippa had imagined, the robe was fake leopard with drawstrings of red ribbon. Philippa tied them around her throat. Wait till Jane saw this!

Philippa paced a few queenly strides around Libby's room. The fake leopard billowed behind her. She drew the collar up to her ears, then looped the robe over one arm and bowed, the way Libby had at the tryouts.

"Ready?" called Mrs. Barber.

Philippa stopped strutting and went back to the living room. "That looks better on you than on me, Philippa," said Libby.

Flattery will get you nowhere, thought Philippa, but she had to keep her face stern to avoid showing pleasure.

Mrs. Barber knelt to pin a new hem. Then she got a needle and thread and basted two darts under Philippa's barely begun bosoms. Philippa saw with abashed surprise that she might have a figure, sort of. "It's fun to give a dress a little pizzazz," said Mrs. Barber. With Abba, things fit or didn't fit. They did not ever have pizzazz.

The front door knocker rattled. Philippa's father opened the door. "Anybody home?" His tone was very friendly, as if he knew he did not even have to use the knocker.

Libby jumped up from the sofa. "Hello, Mr. Cat." Philippa pursed her lips. Mr. Cat?

Philippa's father unbuttoned his overcoat. Libby slipped it from him, as if she did it regularly. "Thanks, Libby, don't hang it up. Can't stay. Hey, Flip, you are surely my princess tonight!" He kissed Philippa's cheek, then leaned over and kissed Mrs. Barber. Philippa watched, her face screwed up with disbelief. She had never seen her father kiss any adult besides an occasional peck at Abba.

Mrs. Barber rose from her knees. "Doesn't Philippa look super, George?"

"You bet," said Philippa's father. Then he linked arms with Libby and smiled at her. "It was nice of Libby to let you wear her dress, Flip." Philippa did not want to be reminded.

Mrs. Barber smoothed the robe over Philippa's shoulders. When her hand slid down Philippa's bare arm, Philippa jerked away. Mrs. Barber looked startled, but she said, "I'll finish the seam and the hem. Stop by Thursday, Philippa. Coffee, George?"

"With cream, sugar," Philippa's father said. Or Philippa thought that was what he said.

Philippa went to Libby's room and took off the costume in such a hurry that she scratched one arm on a pin. There was an awful lot of familiarity around here. It gave Philippa the queer feeling of being an outsider even with her own father.

Fumbling to fasten her belt, Philippa raced downstairs, got both her jacket and her father's coat, and said in a rush, "Thank-you-for-a-lovely-dinner-and-fixing-the-costume. I'm ready to go home, Dad." She waited impatiently while her father finished his coffee.

In the car, her father said, "Nice people, aren't they?"

"Who?"

Her father chuckled. "Janet and Libby."

"Um," said Philippa.

On Thursday, Philippa returned to Sycamore Lane. Libby let her in. The dress and robe, packed into a box, had been left on the coffee table. Philippa put the box under her arm. "Bye," she said.

"Can you stay awhile?" said Libby. "It's so lonely here."

"Where's your grandmother?" asked Philippa.

"Mrs. Bigelow? She's not my grandmother. We can't

afford her too often. Mother telephones from the office, but she doesn't get home till six. We can play backgammon, or cards, if you'd rather."

Philippa knew there was no way she was going to spend an afternoon with Libby. "I can't," said Philippa. "I have homework to do."

"Another time then," said Libby. Didn't she get tired, being so polite all the time?

At the door, Philippa managed to say, "Thanks for the dress and the robe."

"You are quite welcome," said Libby. "You will be stately. Especially if you don't slouch." Philippa squared her shoulders underneath her jacket.

"If you remember not to wave your arms so much the way you did at the tryouts, you will be all right."

All right? Philippa intended to be magnificent! She let the wind whip the door out of her hand so it slammed behind her. Who did Libby think she was, a drama coach or something?

8

On stage at last, Philippa got through "What better use for amethysts . . ." without a single lisp. At the final curtain, Miss Hurholtz murmured, "Good girl."

As parents crowded into the 6-A classroom for refreshments afterward, Philippa accepted compliments with aplomb. Abba had come, as always, looking regal in her hat, and Philippa was pleased she was there. Her father had not come; he was too busy at work to come to school programs, and she did not expect him to. A tiny thought surfaced only once: Wouldn't you have thought Mrs. Barber might have wanted to see how elegant the costume appeared—especially under stage lights and with Philippa in makeup?

Well, she had not come, and nobody wanted her to. The whole idea was stupid.

Later, in the girls' bathroom, Philippa folded the dress

and robe into Mrs. Barber's box. She carried the box home and placed it high on a shelf in her closet.

Weeks later, as Thanksgiving neared, it was still there. By then, Philippa did not think of it. Instead, she was dreading Thanksgiving dinner, for the Catletts had invited the Barbers to join them.

Thanksgiving morning, Philippa's father put two extra leaves in the table. Abba supervised, then said to Philippa, "Did you get the damask napkins out?"

"I forgot." Philippa dug into a drawer in the sideboard. She counted as she piled napkins: "Four for us . . . two for the Bronsons . . . two for Uncle Carroll and Aunt Ellie, that's eight. Two more, Libby and her mother . . . oops." The pile, which she was balancing between arm and stomach, fell to the floor. Philippa knelt to pick them up. Jack crawled out from under the table and left toe-nail marks on the linen heaps.

"Philippa," said Abba, "take that dog out from under foot."

Pop wandered through the dining room, looking for his reading glasses. He dropped a section of the morning paper and failed to notice it. Abba saw it fall and picked it up with a frown. "And your grandfather. Take them both out for a walk."

Philippa found Pop's hat and heavy coat in the hall closet. She held the coat for Pop to put on. As she shrugged into her own jacket, she said, "Jack, walk, boy." Jack rushed to the door.

Philippa waited for Pop to hold her shoulder as he went, sidewise and slow, down the steps. She watched Jack chase Frisk up a tree. "He acts like a puppy," said Philippa, "but he's old enough to've known my mother, isn't he?"

"Huthhay." Birthday, said Pop. He stopped and took out his pad. He gave it to Philippa to hold while he wrote: "Thought you knew. Your mother gave me Jack for a birthday present. They were good friends."

"Yes. That's nice." They walked together slowly.

"You met Dad's friend, Mrs. Barber? You like her, Pop?"

Pop nodded vigorously, even though Mrs. Barber couldn't have given him any birthday present. Philippa felt as unsettled as the November weather. The sun shone between gusted clouds. It was unpleasantly cold. "Let's go home," said Philippa at the end of the block. Pop snapped his fingers at Jack and shuffled around.

Abba had opened the oven and filled the house with savory scents. "What do you suppose Libby's going to eat today?" Philippa asked.

"Parsley, sage, rosemary, and thyme," chanted her father. The doorbell rang, and he was off like a rocket.

It was Uncle Carroll and Aunt Ellie, with their daughter, Mary, and her husband, Scott Bronson. "Where's the girl friend, Georgie?" trumpeted Uncle Carroll.

"Wonder what's keeping Janet?" said her father as he peered out a front window.

"Thought you were, Georgie," said Uncle Carroll. Scott

snorted, but Aunt Ellie hustled him off with a load of coats.

Abba had begun to tut about the turkey being overdone, and Philippa's father was at the telephone when Jack barked at a strange car. It was Mrs. Barber and Libby arriving in a taxi. Over Jack's racket, Mrs. Barber tried to explain that her car would not start. "Then it got so late I called a cab. I'm so sorry." She was as breathless as if she'd run the whole way.

"You should have called me," said Philippa's father. He took her coat and put one arm around her in the process. That did not seem useful to Philippa.

Libby, in a new blue dress, pulled at Philippa's sweater, "Aren't they neat together?" she said.

"What?" said Philippa, and left Libby to Abba. She went into the den where her father had set up bottles. He was pouring sherry for Mrs. Barber. "Steady now," he said in a low voice, "nobody here is going to eat you up," and bent to puff a tiny kiss at her cheek.

Philippa, who scooped up a cube from the ice bucket for something to suck, heard the rest of what he whispered in Mrs. Barber's ear. "Except me," he said, "and I am consuming little nibbles of you every moment." Mrs. Barber got red up to her cheekbones.

Uncle Carroll patted the cushion beside him. "Come sit with me, Janet, and tell me about yourself." Janet left the table of bottles and sat on the couch with Uncle Carroll. As she talked, she fingered her long string of pearls. Philippa's father did not seem to want to do anything except watch her. Philippa coughed quietly, then more loudly.

Her father turned around. "Hi, Flip. Want a ginger ale?"

"Yes," said Philippa.

Her father started to pour martini mix into a glass. "Sorry," he said. "Wrong bottle." He searched for ginger ale.

Philippa held her full glass to her cheek to feel the tiny bubbles explode against her skin. They were like blown kisses. She stood so long her father seemed puzzled. "Did I forget something? Ah, a twist of lemon," and he dropped lemon peel into her glass.

You're forgetting me, Philippa thought.

At the table, Philippa's father dribbled sips of wine into Libby's and Philippa's goblets. "So you can drink a Thanksgiving toast," he said. He lifted his glass. "To the best years of our lives," and everyone drank.

Had they been, or were they coming, Philippa wondered as she tasted. *Brrrr,* whatever the answer, the wine puckered the inside of her mouth something awful. She hurriedly filled her mouth with turkey.

After pumpkin pie, everyone scattered. Philippa's father and Mrs. Barber sat knee to knee as they examined blueprints of a reconstructed building. Though she was curious to see, too, Philippa was rounded up with Libby to clear the table. Libby was so poky, Aunt Ellie took over. Libby said to Philippa, "Shall we play cards, Philippa?"

"How about War?" said Philippa.

Libby giggled. "I think we ought to play Honeymoon Bridge." Libby rolled her eyes at the blueprint sitters. They were very close together.

Nerd, thought Philippa. She gathered more dishes and stacked them in the washer. Libby pressed, "If you don't know how to play Honeymoon Bridge, I can teach you."

To keep Libby quiet, Philippa dragged the card table out of the closet. Libby was explaining the game when Jack, at Pop's feet, let out a piercing whine. Showing the whites of his eyes, he tried to scramble into Pop's lap. Startled, Philippa dropped her cards on the floor.

Body halfway into Pop's lap, Jack sighed and collapsed with his hindquarters draped over Pop's legs. His gray-muzzled head lolled on Pop's good arm, and Pop tried to lift the dog the rest of the way to his lap. He could not, but he held tight and shouted. Abba hurried from the kitchen.

Philippa could not believe what was happening. It was frightening to see Jack so limp. "What's wrong with him . . . is he sick?" whispered Libby.

Philippa's father pushed aside the blueprint and crossed the room. He held a hand first at Jack's nose, then against his chest. He said, "That's it, I think, Pop."

Philippa got up too fast, and her chair toppled. She knelt in front of her grandfather, with the dog pressed between them. She knew her father meant that Jack was dead, but Jack could not be dead. He was warm to her hand, and she let it lay against his body.

Philippa's throat swelled. Her nose began to run. "Is he truly?" she said to her father. He nodded. Philippa stroked Jack's velvet ear and his strong shoulder. She leaned her forehead against Pop's veined hand and let hot tears spill. Jack had been so fast, chasing that squirrel and yipping like a puppy. How could he die just like that?

Through the ache in her throat, Philippa murmured, "Good boy, Jack," and knew some part of her very own life had slipped away. She sobbed a deep, wrenching gulp. A tear dripped from her chin. Jack had left her. Nothing in her life would ever be the same again.

9

In the morning Philippa's father dug a grave beside the rambler rosebush. Philippa found a large rock and with a soft stone wrote "Jack" and the date. She placed it on top of the grave. It did not seem enough, but she did not know what more to do.

Libby telephoned after lunch, to see if Philippa could go to a movie. "How can she talk about movies!" said Philippa.

"She wants to give you something else to think about," said her father.

"I don't want something else to think about," said Philippa. "I want to think about Jack, how he ran and barked and loved hambones . . . everything."

On Monday Philippa moped at school. That week she dropped her lunches, sandwiches with one bite gone, in the trash. Miss Hurholtz watched with concern. At home, Abba said she had to eat some of everything, but mouthfuls stuck in her throat. After school one day she went to visit Jane. Herbert had a new puppy. It was so playful, Philippa could not bear it and climbed the fence home.

Once, Laurie said, "Maybe you can get another dog like Jack."

Philippa said, "There isn't another Jack. If your father died I wouldn't tell you, you could get another like him, would I?"

Thursday afternoon when she was going home from school, she heard Libby call behind her. At first she pretended not to hear. Libby caught up to her. "Philippa, guess what! I called Mother from school. She says we can bake cookies or cupcakes, or whatever you like. Shall we?"

Gloomily, Philippa said, "I never baked anything. Abba doesn't like anyone working in her kitchen but her."

"I've cooked for years," said Libby. "I'll be glad to show you. Mother said to invite you to stay for dinner. Please come."

Philippa started to shake her head, then changed her mind. She guessed whether she suffered at home or at Libby's was hardly important. "Oh, okay," she said. "I'll call Abba from your house."

In the Barbers' small, cheerful kitchen, Libby set out canisters of flour and sugar. Philippa sat on a stool and stared out the window. "Mother said you're the guest, so you get to choose, Philippa. What do you want to bake?"

"Don't know," said Philippa. She thought about how Jack had licked up crumbs under the table.

Libby handed her a fat book. "Here. Mother says this is excellent for beginners."

Philippa opened the book to "Cakes," flipped through pages about measuring and mixing, and landed at: "Wedding & Other Large Cakes." Hastily, she raced over more pages. "Got it," she said. "Fudge Meringue Cake."

Libby looked pained. "I think oatmeal cookies are more—"

"Yahrr," growled Philippa. "Anything but oatmeal. I thought you said I get to choose."

"Yes, of course, but we don't have any chocolate for a Fudge Meringue."

"Oh." Philippa turned to the index.

"If we make cookies, then you can take half of them home."

A good point. "Here's Cookies, then. How about Peanut Butter Delights?" Her squirrel would appreciate a piece.

"Oh, yes, perfect! You measure the brown sugar. I'll measure the white."

"It says beat eggs first," said Philippa. She got two from the refrigerator. Libby got in the way reaching for margarine. Philippa dropped the eggs.

"Oh-h-h-h-h," said Libby.

"Don't worry. I'll clean them up." Philippa threw the bits of shell in the garbage. The yolks wobbled under the sponge and would not sop up. The white was slimy and stretched. Libby got a large spoon. Together, they chased the eggs into a corner where Libby could scrape the strings of white and yellow into a dustpan.

"Mother says a kitchen floor just about needs washing every day anyway," said Libby. "Let's not waste time cleaning now. We can mop after we bake."

Philippa beat the second batch of eggs in a large red bowl, while Libby exclaimed over Philippa's measure of brown sugar. "You don't know how to measure brown sugar, Philippa."

"I do, too. It's an exact half."

"Mother says brown sugar is different. It has to be pressed into the cup. See?" Libby firmed the fluff of brown with the flat of a knife. The half cup shrank to nothing.

Philippa shook flour into a marked pint. This time, she pressed down heavily with her spoon several times. Flour spouted like a fountain. Billows of white settled on the counter tops.

"No, no, no," shrieked Libby. "Mother says never pack flour." She grabbed Philippa's cup to dump the flour back into its canister.

"Hey!" said Philippa.

"Spoon it carefully, so it stays fluffy. Mother says you can shake the cup gently to settle it."

Mother says. Philippa yawned. Why had she let herself into this boring afternoon with this boring girl? Philippa pressed her hand into the open flour canister, lifted it, and looked at the handprint she had made. Each finger was outlined; the palm was perfect.

Libby said, "What are you doing, Philippa?"

Philippa put her other hand in the top of the flour. She held up both palms. "Ladyfingers," she said.

"Mother says—"

Philippa eyed Libby's dark-blue turtleneck. "Mother says GO," she said. *Pluffft*, she placed her right hand on the right side of Libby's chest. Then *pluffft*, she placed her left hand on the left side. The prints showed up beautifully on the navy blue.

"Stop it, Philippa!"

"It's a game like Simon Says. Mother Says, turn around and I'll decorate your back."

"I do not want my back decorated."

"You have to say 'Mother Says, I don't want to be decorated,' if you want me not to do it," said Philippa. She grabbed and printed Libby's shoulder lopsidedly.

"*I* want you not to do it," said Libby.

Philippa floured her hands again and feinted at Libby. Libby, eyes glittering, whacked her on the forearm with the flat of the knife she had used to measure margarine. Grease spread on Philippa's sweater. Philippa stepped backward and skidded in egg white. Libby whacked at her again, but Philippa caught her hand and forced it upward. "Say, 'Mother Says no fighting,'" Philippa said.

Libby's chest heaved. Her strong ballet legs wrapped around Philippa's legs. Off balance, they tumbled to the floor. "Oof," said Libby. Philippa's elbow had jabbed her in the middle.

Philippa rolled off Libby and sat up. "If you'd stop acting silly," she said, "we could get these cookies cooked."

"You are sillier than anybody," said Libby. She got up.

"Where's the peanut butter?" said Philippa. She left floury fingerprints as she hunted on several shelves.

"Naturally, it is in the refrigerator," said Libby. "It is all natural because it comes from Jolly Joan's where they only have natural foods and no preservatives."

"That place," said Philippa. "It seemed real un-natural to me." She took the jar from the refrigerator and banged it down beside Libby's measure of milk. The milk jiggled and dripped a white line down the blue-painted counter to the floor. "Another measly puddle is nothing," Philippa pointed out.

"You are very messy," observed Libby. Her hand shook as she poured salt, and the grains crunched under their feet.

When the dough was ready, they took turns dropping spoonfuls in rows on cookie sheets. Then Libby discovered she had forgotten to turn on the oven. She was vexed. "Mother says always turn on the stove in advance."

Philippa fingered a cookie blob waiting to be baked. She picked out a raisin and ate it. Tasty. She stuck a thumb into the dough and sucked it clean.

"Mother says raw flour isn't good for you." Libby bent to the temperature gauge at the front of the stove. The seat of her jeans, where it said "Calvin," was a temptation.

Philippa scooped up a cookie and threw. The lump stuck to the denim. Libby stood erect. "What are you doing now, Philippa?"

"Nothing." Philippa felt a giggle rising in her chest. She had not giggled since Thanksgiving.

"This oven heats very slowly," said Libby, "not like the one we had in Buffalo." She sat on the stool to wait and sensed the slidy-ness of dough under one buttock. Philippa burst into laughter at the look on Libby's face.

Libby's cheeks flamed with anger. Scraping a hand across her jeans, Libby rolled the dough into a ball and threw it at Philippa. Philippa ducked, and the dough hit the windowpane. It slid a little, then stuck. Libby reached for another blob from the cookie sheet and tried to slap it on Philippa's head. Shaking with laughter, Philippa grabbed a spoonful of dough from the bowl and, fending off Libby with one arm, flicked the spoonful with the other. Splat. She missed Libby but got the refrigerator.

"There!" said Libby triumphantly as she ground Peanut Butter Delight into Philippa's part.

"Libby!"

The girls untwisted themselves from one another. Libby was breathing fast. Philippa could not stop laughing. Libby's mother, in her navy jacket and scarf, stood in the doorway. "Mother!" said Libby. "We never heard you come in."

"Mm," said Janet Metz-Barber. She gazed at the floor. Eggy footsteps led from the refrigerator to the sink to the stove. She glanced at the dough plastered to the refrigerator, then at the oval bump on the window. Philippa waited for the gust of righteous anger that would have exploded from Abba. Mrs. Barber only unbuttoned her coat, very, very slowly. It was so quiet you could hear the oven click with heat.

"If there is any dough left to bake, you'd best bake it," said Mrs. Barber.

"We were playing a game," said Philippa, "like, uh, mixing things up."

Mrs. Barber's eyebrows quirked. "You are very good at mixing things up," she said. Her voice was frosty.

Libby slid both cookie sheets in the oven. "I am terribly sorry about the floor," she said. "We were going to clean it so you'd never know we broke the eggs." She twitched a damp sponge around the flour on the counter top.

"Strange how making a mess can seem so hilarious," said her mother. "I can see you two had a splendid time." Her upper lip curled with sarcasm at the word "splendid."

"It wasn't all Libby's fault, the throwing," said Philippa. She was amazed at herself. "I mean, I invented this game, and I got a little flour on Libby, so—" Philippa gestured at the window lump.

"Get the mop and the pail from the garage," said Mrs. Barber to Libby. Then to Philippa, "What game exactly?"

"It was kind of feeble."

"Yes?"

"It was Mother Says. Like Simon Says."

Mrs. Barber pulled up the stool with the toe of one boot, brushed off a raisin, and sat down. She cradled her chin in one hand. " 'Mother Says'. Mmhm, I know how Libby talks. Were you taunting Libby? Was that what you were doing?"

"Well," said Philippa. She shrugged.

"So it was a bitter gibe, and Libby is so vulnerable." Philippa shifted her weight from one foot to the other.

"You know, *mother* isn't an empty word. It stands for a person."

"Oh, sure, sure," said Philippa, but she grinned as she remembered the first *pluffft* she had delivered on Libby's shirt.

Mrs. Barber winced at the grin. "I wish, Philippa, that you would stop venting anger, intended for me, on Libby."

"I don't know what you're talking about," muttered Philippa.

"Libby would like to like you. So would I." Philippa looked sullenly at the dirty floor. She could not tell her footprints from Libby's on the tiles.

Mrs. Barber rose from the stool. "However, at the moment, I do not think I like you at all. Libby does not need to be made fun of. And *I* do not appreciate your doing so. Cruelty is never necessary. I think you can go home now."

Home! Sent home like a naughty three-year-old? Philippa stared Mrs. Barber in the eye. Philippa was not afraid of anybody's little mother.

Mrs. Barber stared right back. "I think you lack discipline. If you were my child, I would send you to your room. Since you are not, I send you home to your grand-mother. Go, girl, before I lose my cool."

When Philippa moved very slowly, Mrs. Barber thrust her face close to Philippa's. She breathed, "Scat! Mother Says!"

10

Once she was well away from the Barber house and no one could see her, Philippa broke into a run. Granules of cookie dough dropped from her hair. She stopped briefly to brush them loose. Philippa's nose was dripping, and she shivered with cold. Home seemed miles away.

There was an eerie shadow cloaking the front of the house when Philippa reached it. She was not expected home so early, and so no one had turned on the porch light for her.

Philippa saw in the glow of the kitchen lights that Abba and Pop were eating at the small table. The two of them seemed so cozy without her. Philippa hugged her arms in the dark.

Abba was going to be floored when her granddaughter walked in at this hour. "And *why* were you sent home, Phil-lip-puh?" Abba was going to say. Philippa knew how her eyes tended to widen with displeasure.

What Philippa wanted to answer was: Because those Barbers are real turds, that's why. But not to Abba would she ever say that.

It would be nice if Abba were angry at Mrs. Barber for sending a poor hungry child into the night, but in her heart, Philippa knew otherwise. Abba would press for details and only be angry with Philippa. Would she be angry with Philippa!

Through the shadowy garden, Philippa kept on going. She swung over the fence and skitted past the dark school, where the fire escapes loomed like dinosaurs. Jane's friendly, lighted house was just beyond.

Philippa stood by the Overrackers' dining room window. The family sat around a large table, two adults and five children. She could hear their voices through the glass, especially Mr. Overracker's. Laughter shook his immense shoulders. Though Abba discouraged visits, Philippa had eaten there a few times. Mrs. Overracker had a freezer full of dinners, and the kids put them in the oven while she was at work.

Mrs. Overracker sat with her back to the kitchen. She was ladling dripping portions of something yellowish out of a huge dish. It looked like macaroni and cheese. Philippa's mouth seemed to spring a leak. She swallowed. Since lunch she'd had nothing to eat except a taste of peanut butter cookies, raw at that. Besides, she had not had any appetite since Jack died.

She watched Jane's mother hand a plate to Herbert. She moved closer to the window. Philippa thought about how macaroni and cheese bubbled up in a pot like that, how the crust formed brown and crunchy on the surface, how oozy it was underneath. Her stomach growled. She pressed close to the glass.

Philippa saw Mrs. Overracker pass salad to Mindy and suddenly rise from the table. She slipped through the kitchen and opened the door to peer outside. "Hi," said Philippa. "It's me. Philippa." Herbert's puppy dashed out to wriggle around her ankles.

"So it is," said Jane's mother. "Come in, love, and have a bite. It's cold out there." She asked no questions about what Philippa was doing, spying on them almost.

Philippa went in. It was macaroni and cheese. "Phil?" said Jane. "Hi."

"Get another plate," said Mrs. Overracker.

Amber started to say, "Haven't you had din—"

Mrs. Overracker interrupted. "Philippa can always eat a little macaroni and cheese. Another chair, Denise."

Philippa polished off a big helping. "It's awful good, thank you." Mrs. Overracker reached over with another ladleful.

Mindy rose before the rest were through. "I'm late for rehearsal," she said. Mindy had a part in a high school play.

"You'll be a little later," her father said. "As I recall, your job is to clear and wash."

Mindy groaned. "Oh, if you people would just buy a dishwasher like everybody else. I'll do the dishes when I get home."

"That's too late, Mindy. You know you'll never get to school on time in the morning." Mrs. Overracker was firm, but Philippa could not hear Abba's tone of indignation.

"Nuts," said Mindy.

"Do not speak to your mother that way," roared Mr. Overracker. His chest swelled so much Philippa remembered a picture of a bull elephant pulling up trees.

Philippa got prickles along her spine, but Mindy was not entirely fazed. "You expect me to act like a household slave or something."

"Your mother works hard, and I expect you to help at home," said Mr. Overracker. "You can help your mother, or you can get lost."

"John," said Mrs. Overracker.

Philippa stopped chewing. Nobody else's jaws worked either. Mindy was as tense as a coiled spring.

Mr. Overracker burst into loud chuckles. Tension dissolved like the cheese in the sauce. "Okay, Mindy," Mr. Overracker said, "you can do some before you go, 'cause I'll help, and maybe somebody else will volunteer, too."

"Me," said Philippa. "I'll be glad to." She was so relieved Mindy was not left with the choice of getting lost.

"Thanks, Philippa," said Mindy, kissing her father good-bye. "You and Jane can come to the dress rehearsal if you want."

Later, Jane took a flashlight to walk Philippa to the fence. "What's up, Phil?" she said when they'd picked their way through toys abandoned on the sidewalk.

"I went to Libby's after school. We made some cookies. Then Libby's mother got really grossed out at me," Philippa said. "She told me to go home."

"What for? What did you do?" said Jane.

"Nothing much. She doesn't have a sense of humor like your father does. She thought I was making fun of Libby."

"Were you?"

"Some. It's easy. Then she mixed dough in my hair. Her mother didn't notice that very much."

Jane had the light aimed at the fence. "What are you going to tell your grandmother?"

"What she doesn't know won't hurt her," said Philippa.

"But what'll I tell my mom . . . why you were at our house without dinner?"

Philippa paused near the fence. "I didn't think she minded. How come she didn't ask me, just invited me in?"

"That's Mom's way. She thinks anybody in trouble first needs a square meal. If she finds somebody peeking through her window, she feeds first and asks afterward. She'll ask *me*. She wouldn't want to have embarrassed you."

"So tell her the truth," said Philippa. "Your mother's all right, you know what I mean?" She climbed the fence and hurried up the path along the grape arbor. She went into the house quickly.

"Hi," yelled Philippa. "I'm home."

Abba put down the telephone, *clack*. Her mouth was

drawn down and her eyebrows up. "And where have you been?" Abba said.

Philippa did not look at Abba as she unzipped her jacket. Something had gone wrong. Abba knew.

"I want to know where you have been. Your father is combing the streets for you. I was going to phone the police. Young lady, account for yourself."

That Barber witch must have squealed. "You said I could have dinner at Libby's."

"But you did not have dinner there. Pop and I have been worried sick about you. You have been gallivanting, thoughtless and feckless."

Pop stood in the kitchen doorway. He held out his good arm. "Fffpp. Hoo hawhye?" Flip, you all right?

"Sure, Pop." She hugged him. "I had dinner at the Overrackers' instead."

Abba sizzled. "The Over-rack-ers. How many times have I told you I do not like to have you in that dreadful neighborhood. Why didn't you come straight home from Libby's?"

Philippa answered anger with anger. "Don't give me that snooty stuff, Abba. I had dinner and it was delicious. Nobody asked me to account for being there or asked why I was there when I wasn't invited or anything. Only get another plate and pull up another chair. You're too mean to understand people who are generous and, and . . ." She unleashed a sob. "And ni-i-i-ice," but this came out a wail.

Philippa dashed for the stairs, and once in her room, threw herself on her bed. She cried wetly though briefly. She could not afford to cry very long. She needed to know when her father got home and what he had to say when he came in. She blew her nose, then crept to the head of the stairs to listen.

11

After what seemed like a very long time, Philippa heard her father. His voice was anxious. "No luck," he said.

"Your daughter is home," said Abba. "She never thought to tell us she was hobnobbing with those people on the other side of the school."

"Whew! I'm glad she's home," said Philippa's father. "Where is she?"

Before Abba could say "upstairs," Philippa tiptoed to her bed.

Abba also said, "The child is irresponsible. You need to talk to her, George." Philippa could hear him take the steps two at a time. Her heart thumped in anticipation.

Her father entered her room and sat on the side of her bed. He massaged between her shoulder blades for a minute. "You had me frightened," he said. "I'm glad you're all right, Flip."

Silence from Philippa.

After a moment her father said, "You could have been more considerate of Abba and Pop."

More silence.

"As far as I can tell, almost everybody in this mixup has been inconsiderate of the other person's feelings. Janet feels bad because she was not more understanding of your problems."

Surprised, Philippa sat up. "I don't have any problems. What are you—she—talking about?" She hugged the pillow. That dumb woman.

"Ah," said her father, " 'your motherless child' Janet said to me. She meant to be kinder to you, and Libby was very unhappy you went home."

"I don't want anything from those dippy Barbers," said Philippa.

"Hm," said her father, "but I want something from you, kiddo . . . understanding and appreciation of other people's feelings, okay? I think the Barbers and the Catletts should get together and tell each other we're sorry about the misunderstanding or whatever it was."

"Abba's part of the misunderstanding, too!" said Philippa.

"I fail to see how your grandmother had anything to do with your leaving the Barbers' house and having dinner at the other house."

"You don't understand!" said Philippa. "It's mostly Abba's fault, see. She never let me bake anything, so I didn't know how to measure stuff right. I had to do it over and over. Libby kept telling me 'Mother says' and then we threw the cookies around a little. Libby's mother said to go home and I went. Then Abba hadn't left a light on, so I climbed the fence because it looked like they didn't want me here and I went to the street she doesn't like and they gave me—"

"Stop!" said her father. "Enough!" He held his hands over his ears and laughed a little, helplessly.

Philippa spoke more slowly. "Abba is a snooty snob. She hates it because Jane's mom works in the diner. Mrs. Overracker is much nicer than Abba, I think, and—"

Said her father sternly, "Cut it out, Flip. You know that Abba loves you very much."

Philippa growled as much like Jack as she possibly could, but her father took no notice. "Abba was worried about what had happened to you. Pop, too. However, I'm sure the Overrackers are good people, or you wouldn't like them. I'll settle that with your grandmother for you."

"Thanks, Dad," said Philippa. She started to slide off the bed.

"Wait a sec," said her father. "Sit down. I'm not finished. There are a couple more things I want to talk about. First, I want you always to remember to let me or Abba know where you are. I thought we understood that."

"Sure. Okay," said Philippa. "I only forgot this once."

She yawned. She sank against her father's wool-smelling shoulder. Her father put his arm around her and said, "You don't remember your mother, do you?"

"Uh-uh." She shook her head. There was only that scary dream that came in the night sometimes.

"I have her picture on my bureau," her father said. Philippa knew the photograph. It was in a silver frame and showed a young woman with a straight nose and a broad mouth like Philippa's. The photo had a name, Nancy Catlett.

"I thought, maybe Janet Barber might think enough of me, of us, to become a mother to you, Flip."

Mrs. Barber be a *mother* to her? "No! Not Libby's mother!" shouted Philippa. She sat upright, eyes wide, her hands in fists. Her stomach was in a knot.

"Sure. Think about it. Being together would be good for all four of us. That's one reason we should get together and make future plans after we smooth out any misunderstandings."

"What do you mean 'future plans'?" Philippa sat rigid with shock.

Philippa's father tried to pry her clenched fingers apart so that he could hold her hand. Philippa moved away from him.

Her father took no notice and went on. "Making future plans means we can talk about sharing households so Libby would be company for you. You would be company for her. I think only children tend to be lonely children."

"EN . . . OH . . . NO! I'm not lonely," said Philippa. "There's everybody here I want to live with."

"But no mother," her father said. "When your mother died in that accident, it was a very tragic time. I knew someday you'd need more than just a father."

"A father is plenty," said Philippa. "A father is okay." This time she let her father take her hand.

"It's nice you think so," he said. "I have some exciting news, too. I told you we were looking at that building on Commerce Street? Well, Roy and I bought it."

"That scungy place near the health food store?"

"It's a good solid building. One of the reasons Janet came to work with us is because she has had experience redesigning old buildings. We're getting a lot of that kind of work these days. She's drawn plans for two floors of office space and developed the two top floors for an apartment. We can live there and be very happy."

Philippa knew he did not intend Pop, with his bad leg, to live up a bunch of stairs, but she did not want to face the fact that she knew it. "Who's going to live there?" she asked.

"Me, for one."

"Then *you* will be lonesome," Philippa said.

Her father gazed at her levelly. "I expect my daughter to live with me," he said. "I want the four of us—Janet, Libby, you, and I—to take over the apartment in the new building."

"Wha-a-at?"

"Sure. I'd like to marry Janet. She cares about me, you see, but she can't see her way clear to marriage right now. If we share our families and the space . . ."

"Gross!"

"Not gross, Flip. Great. Then if Janet decides someday to marry me, we will already have had lots of experience."

"Experience in what?"

Her father's forehead twitched. "Well, loving and living together and being kind to one another, like being married but not quite."

Philippa put her hands on her knees and looked her father up and down. "Married but not quite? Isn't that kind of—funny? What does Abba say about that?"

Her father laughed wryly. "A lot and all of it loud. Abba can change her old-fashioned notions, but even if she doesn't, I have a right, and so does Janet, to do what we know is best. And I'll tell you, kitten, Abba has always wanted what is best for you. I know she wants you to have a mother."

Philippa felt cold. She held her arms across her stomach and remembered how left-out she had felt that night she tried on the costume at 22 Sycamore. "You talked to everybody before you talked to me."

"Only to Abba, and of course Janet. I want to know how you feel about it, and . . ."

Philippa leaped off the bed. "I think it's a lousy, rotten, dumb idea! Don't you stick me with that nerd, Libby; and that witch isn't my mother. Don't you ever call her

86

my mother, ever, ever. Mrs. Barber can't stand me, and I can't stand her. I have my own mother, somewhere, and I don't need somebody else's, even if you think so. I know she's not here, and Jack isn't here with me anymore either, but they're still mine. My mother put me into blankets in a sled and she k-kissed me on the cheek." The words were tumbling out, and Philippa's heart drummed with the absolute, sudden remembering.

"My mother loved me." Philippa stopped. Her father's eyes were so stricken, Philippa wanted to hug him. Almost. He loved her, too, didn't he? Then why—?

"Ugh!" said Philippa. She might have felt the same if a hockey stick had caught her in the middle—breathless and sore. She realized that the real meaning in this entire mishmash of words was that her father loved Janet Barber.

Her father sighed. "You're right. Your mother loved you, and I loved your mother. I did not understand you felt so strongly."

Philippa wiped her nose on the back of her hand. Her father smiled. "We don't have to settle everything tonight. A new idea takes getting used to. We must think of Abba's life, too. She's getting older, and she deserves a little rest."

Philippa's eyes stung with tears. "I don't ever want to leave this house. This is our house, mine and yours and Pop and Abba's. It's where I want to live until I'm grown up."

Her father rubbed one hand up and down his jaw. "I'm

sorry I've upset you. Remember, though, this is Abba and Pop's house, not truly ours. I want us to have ours. Now let's go down so you can tell Abba you're sorry you worried her, all right?"

In her bed that night, Philippa went over the scene with her father. There was so much for her to think about, including what she had never expressed before—that her mother had loved her. It was weird how she had liked saying it. She whispered it again in the dark. "My mother loved me." With that, exhausted with the day's ups and downs, Philippa fell asleep immediately.

The next day at school, Philippa kept returning to painful thoughts the way her tongue might lick a hurt spot on her lip. She had to find out what Libby knew.

After lunch, she offered Libby a piece of bubble gum. "Thank you," said Libby. "My moth—the dentist, that is, says chewing gum is terrible for the teeth, but I like it." She put the piece in her mouth.

Philippa surprised herself by saying, "Sorry about the game and the fight and everything yesterday."

"It's all right," said Libby. She tried to blow a bubble.

"You got to chew more before it's ready," said Philippa. "Wait till the sugar's out."

Libby giggled. "The sugar you measured was funny yesterday."

"You sitting on the cookie dough was kind of funny, too."

Libby laughed. "I would have brought you your share

of the cookies, but Mother and I had such a disagreement after you ran out that we forgot the oven. The cookies burned to cinders. We'll have to bake some more. We had fun, didn't we?"

"Is that what it was?" said Philippa. Then she remembered that she had been laughing when they'd thrown stuff at each other.

"Overall, I think it was. I told Mother she is too protective of me. You know how they are sometimes."

"Abba's awful that way. Eat this, eat that." They chewed comfortably together.

Libby blew a fairly decent bubble. "Did you see that, Philippa?"

"Neat," said Philippa. She blew a bigger one.

Still, Philippa needed to find out what Libby knew, or if she knew. "My father said the four of us should talk about getting along together. What does your mother think about that?"

Libby shook her head. "I do not wish to find out. Mother and I are not yet speaking fully to one another. There is that smell of burning in the entire house. Every time Mother breathes deeply I can see she remembers she lost her temper and sent you away, and it bothers her. We should let bygones be bygones, I think."

"Okay with me," said Philippa generously.

12

Philippa's father arranged for a special meeting to be held in Abba's living room. He and Philippa, Abba and Pop, Janet and Libby, were to have "a serious conversation."

During dinner that night, Abba frowned like a thundercloud. The mashed potatoes were scorched; the gravy lacked salt. "Ma," said George Catlett, "relax. There's no need to worry so much over nothing."

"It's not 'nothing,'" said Abba. "It's your life, George, and Philippa's, and oh, what will people think?"

"Let them think as they like and tend to their knitting," said Philippa's father, "and we'll tend to ours."

Philippa thought that was what Abba would like—needles to stick into everyone. Her father said, "I hear Janet's car outside. Behave yourself, Ma."

Philippa had never known anyone tell Abba to behave herself. Hearing steps on the porch, Philippa opened the front door before Libby'd had time to ring the bell. Libby smiled. "This is so exciting," she breathed in Philippa's ear as she passed. How much does she know? Philippa wondered.

Mrs. Barber seemed very businesslike. She wore a gray flannel suit and a white blouse. Philippa had not seen her since the night she had said, "Scat, Mother Says." Uneasy, Philippa moved to the opposite side of the room and sat on the arm of Pop's chair. She watched Mrs. Barber out of the corners of her eyes for any further evidence of unfriendliness. At each glance from Philippa, Mrs. Barber tried a smile; once she started to extend a hand. Philippa stuck with Pop and did not smile in return.

Mrs. Barber perched on the edge of Abba's antique piano stool. Philippa's father patted the empty space on the sofa beside him, but Mrs. Barber shook her head and stayed where she was. Libby sat on the floor, on a cushion by her mother's boots.

Abba, who'd gone to the kitchen to leave her apron, was the last to enter the room. Philippa could tell that Abba had brushed her hair and put on some lipstick, but she was not welcoming. Abba sat bolt upright, in one of great-grandmother's wedding chairs.

Philippa's father cleared his throat and leaned forward. Rather formally, he began: "Janet and I think it is time we get together and talk. I have asked Janet to marry me. At this point she feels she can't. She's been through a lot. The divorce and custody battles were too painful."

⚓
91

All heads turned toward little Mrs. Barber. Abba seemed to glare. Everyone else, Philippa thought, was more curious than anything. For herself, though she did not want her father to marry anyone, she thought Mrs. Barber was an airhead not to want to marry him.

Under Abba's direct gaze, Mrs. Barber folded her hands and crossed her legs. The toe of one boot vibrated slightly, and her knuckles showed white. Why, thought Philippa, she's scared of Abba.

"We are going to join households," said Philippa's father. "The new apartment above our business offices will be very comfortable for a family of four."

"It is, of course, more efficient," offered Mrs. Barber. There seemed to be a slight tremble as she said *efficient.*

Abba went *humph,* and Pop drew "efficient" on his pad, then underlined it.

"That is," said Mrs. Barber, "it is easier to care for a family and do a full day's work at the same time." She crossed her legs the other way and half-smiled in Philippa's direction. Philippa leaned her cheek against Pop's bald spot.

"I should think the family came first," objected Abba.

"Yes, exactly," said Philippa's father. "Our families do come first. Janet and I want Libby and Flip with us because then we are a family. When we live and work together, family living is a reality. It isn't when we live apart. That's clear, I think."

Abba said, "I do not see why a simple wedding in the grape arbor in June is so difficult."

"No," said Mrs. Barber. "I am not ready for that. Marriage has been too painful for me, if you can understand that, Grace. The divorce from Holden was shattering—I could never go through anything like that again."

"Don't worry, Mother," said Libby.

"Who's Holden?" said Philippa.

"My father," said Libby softly.

"You see, Ma," said Philippa's father, "we are going to play it by ear, so to speak. We will work in the building we live in because we want our children with us."

"Permanent arrangements can be left for future consideration," said Mrs. Barber. She was back to sounding businesslike, and Philippa was glad of it. As far as Philippa was concerned, if it wasn't "permanent," then it had to be temporary, and temporary was like a sleepover, here today and gone tomorrow. She could put up with that for a while.

"Children adapt well to changes when the adults agree to implement them," said Mrs. Barber to Abba. "I am sure you want what's best for Philippa."

"Certainly!" wrote Pop, and flapped his pad toward Abba.

"It seems so farfetched," said Abba, "not to speak of faraway. That neighborhood doesn't seem safe."

Philippa pricked up her ears. If Abba did not like a neighborhood, there must be something really interesting about it. Abba did not like Jane's street, and there was something going on there every minute.

"Commerce Street—that whole area—is in a state of flux," said Philippa's father. "Plenty of changes going on there. We're moving in, and there will be others. A motel will be finished by summer. It has a swimming pool we can use. You have to get used to changing times, Ma."

Mrs. Barber said brightly, "I think you will see that the girls will have more of a chance to grow up and expand their horizons. For instance, we'll all share the household responsibilities."

"Philippa and I can bake cookies," said Libby, and clapped a hand over her mouth.

"Yes, and other things as well," said Libby's mother. For the first time since entering the Catletts' living room, Mrs. Barber smiled a full, warm smile. It was as if the sun flashed through the storm clouds that hung in the air. Philippa's father smiled, too, then rose and hugged Mrs. Barber. Abba sighed. Philippa's mouth dropped open. "Love . . . Love . . . Love" sang an ancient recording in her head.

Libby put a hand on her mother's knee. She said, "It will be all right, Mother. I know it will."

"Thanks, sweetie. We need your love and support, and Philippa's, too. Philippa, will you call me Janet?"

"No!" said Philippa. Her father's face fell two feet. For his sake, Philippa tried to sound less hostile. "Mrs. Barber is fine."

Pop doodled a sad face on his pad.

"It seems so formal," said Mrs. Barber. She didn't have to pretend to be so unhappy, Philippa thought.

"Can I call Mr. Cat, 'George'?" said Libby.

"Of course," said Philippa's father. He looked at Philippa. She scowled as darkly as she could.

On Saturday morning, when she had time to herself, Philippa wondered if she'd been bamboozled into this new living arrangement. It was clear that a decision had been made, and that she and Libby were a part of it.

She loved her father, and she was going to live at 102 Commerce Street because he wanted her there. But she did not believe anybody expected her to love the Barbers. Just living in the same house with them seemed like walking through a field with poison ivy in it.

Philippa gravitated to the attic. Staring out the little octagonal window, she saw her father get into his car with the fixed fender and drive away. Philippa balanced herself on the edge of a chair with a broken seat. She put her elbows on her knees and rested her chin on her fists. Love and sex and the rest of that stuff: It was a *PG* script or maybe an *R*. She closed her eyes and tried to imagine her father and Mrs. Barber doing it together. Yuck. The stupid reasons adults thought up to rearrange everybody's lives. None of it seemed good enough to leave Frisk in the maple tree and Jack under the rosebush and Abba and Pop. If you added it up, there were more people here to love her than at Commerce Street.

Unless, unless . . . what was it Dad had said about Abba deserving a rest? Philippa's blood ran to icewater, and her heart sank into her sneakers.

Philippa ran downstairs. Abba was in the living room,

a dustcloth in one hand and a bottle of lemon oil furniture cream in the other. "Abba," said Philippa, "you and Pop are tired of me."

"Such nonsense," said Abba. "Children are expected to live with their parents, that's all." She did not look at Philippa, only kept wiping and squirting lemon cream.

"You think I'm too noisy, and I argue too much," said Philippa, "but arguing is like thinking out loud to me. I promise to practice being more thoughtful and not get into any arguments. Let me stay, and I'll be very quiet."

"Dear me," said Abba. She let the dust cloth dangle.

Philippa's voice quavered. "I want to stay here with you and Pop. I don't want to live with those other people. You wouldn't send me away if you really loved me."

"Oh-oh!" said Abba. Her face crumpled, and she sat on the sofa. She held out her arms. "My baby, Philippa." Philippa threw herself into her grandmother's lap. The sofa creaked. Philippa hung on to Abba, and Abba hung on to Philippa.

Pop came in. "Hah's hoin on?" What's going on, he said.

Philippa gulped. "I won't leave if you don't want me to, Pop," she said. Pop grunted and eased himself into his chair.

"The child thinks we want her to leave," said Abba. She wiped her eyes with the dust cloth.

"Heheh!" Never! Pop pounded the arm of his chair.

"Janet Barber wants to be a mother to you, dear. I can

only hope in time Janet will agree to legalize this household. You will want to live with your father, but you can visit us any time."

"I'll visit them," said Philippa, "and I'll stay here."

"Hoh," said Pop.

"What do you mean 'no'?" said Philippa. She left Abba's lap to sit on Pop's footstool.

"It's not like they're getting married or anything permanent, so why do *I* have to figure anything permanent?"

Abba snorted and stood up. "*Humph.* She has something there. This kind of moving in together without the benefit of clergy . . ." Abba clucked her tongue.

Pop pounded the arm of his chair even harder. "Hayce!" Grace! he scolded.

"I know, I know, G. H." Abba shook her head. "In my day, when two people felt toward each other the way George and Janet do, you got married and that was that."

"No, no," said Philippa. "I'm glad they're not getting married. I don't want to live with Libby forever."

"That's the one decent thing about it," said Abba firmly. "You and Libby will be good for one another. But dear, you have to go where your father goes. That is how life is. But wait. I've been thinking. I want you to have those sterling silver bud vases and the cut glass fruit compote. I was going to give them to you when you're older, but you take them now. And I've always meant for you to have your great-grandmother's wedding chairs."

"Abba, what am I going to do with a bunch of antiques?"

"I want you to have some of my lovely things. Let's see, that Dresden plate quilt, I have always saved for—"

"Abba, cut it out," yelled Philippa.

"Don't speak to me like that," said Abba.

They glared at one another. Philippa was the first to smile. "Why are we always fighting, Abba?"

"Because we are so much alike, dear. Now don't make anything more difficult for Pop and me. It is just tearing us apart to let you go, but you must go where your father thinks best."

A tear trickled down Philippa's cheek. Pop gently rubbed it away with his forefinger. Philippa sniffled and stood up.

"There," said Abba. "How tall you've become." She put both arms about Philippa and hugged her tight. Philippa buried her head in that nice spot at Abba's neckline. They rocked in silence together.

"It is nice to be tall," Abba said. "Your mother was tall, you know."

"Oh?" said Philippa. "Mrs. Barber is so little."

"Ah, well," said her grandmother, "I think there was only one Nancy for George, only one." Philippa knew that was a very comforting thought.

"And truthfully," said Abba, "I am *so* glad George found someone to love again, Philippa. You will understand when you are older."

98

"Just you and Pop love *me*, that's all I want," said Philippa.

Pop smiled and took out his pad and pen: "Forever," he wrote. He tore off the paper and tucked it into Philippa's back pocket.

13

One January afternoon, Mrs. Barber drove Abba, Philippa, and Libby downtown for the first view of 102 Commerce Street. Abba said, "I used to think George needed a nice home in the suburbs." Then she lowered her voice. "My dear, you two ought to get married. People expect it."

Mrs. Barber said heatedly, "Yes, and then the same people delight in the divorce case when it doesn't work out." The light turned green, and she gunned the motor. The car shot forward.

In front of the brownstone was a small paved courtyard. It contained a fountain basin filled with dead leaves. When they got out of the car, Philippa plucked a burlap sack from a mound and discovered a naked cherub with a pitcher, designed to pour water into the basin.

"Abba," said Philippa, "you'll like this. We have an antique fountain."

Abba glanced at the cherub. "A true Victorian statue would display a fig leaf," she said. "That must be modern."

"Well," said Mrs. Barber cheerfully, "we'll be a very modern addition to the building ourselves. This house was built in eighteen seventy-eight. It has such possibilities, don't you think so?"

Abba was persistent. "For the children's sake, I should think—"

Mrs. Barber cut her off. "No mental fig leaves! We will be happy being honest with one another from the beginning."

Abba was silent. Philippa slowly climbed a flight of steps. For the first time, she saw that Janet Barber could stand up to Abba, whether she was scared of her or not.

They went through a double door of frosted glass into the apartment. A paint cloth covered the vestibule radiator. There was a smell of plaster and new lumber. "Watch your step," said Mrs. Barber. Abba, Philippa noticed with a grin, instead of looking to her feet, stared at the ceiling as if it were going to fall.

"Is that lighting fixture crooked?" Abba said.

The stairs to the bedrooms enchanted Libby. "A curving staircase!" she exclaimed. "Wouldn't it be elegant to sweep down that in a gown with a train?"

"A wedding gown," said Abba.

Mrs. Barber disappeared down the hall.

They followed her to see the kitchen, which Mrs. Barber had redesigned. "There will be a deck out there, with stairs to the garden below," she pointed out. "Sliding glass doors will let in the sunlight."

"Won't soot from the railroad seep through?" said Abba.

"The doors are self-sealing," said Mrs. Barber. "Here's the living room. We're knocking out a wall to enlarge the space."

"Drafty," said Abba, and drew her fur collar close to her chin.

"Where's *my* room?" said Philippa. "Can we go upstairs?"

"Of course," said Mrs. Barber.

Philippa and Libby started up the staircase, side by side, but at the curve where the stairs narrowed, Philippa squeezed past Libby and reached the top floor first.

Mrs. Barber waited for Abba, then she closed in on Philippa. "You and Libby have rooms on the south side of the house. Each is the same size. Your bath is between with a door from each room."

Philippa stopped suddenly. "One bathroom? I got to share a bathroom?" At home she shared with her father, but that was different.

"I don't mind," said Libby. Nobody was asking her!

"A bath is a very expensive unit," said Mrs. Barber. "We can't afford one for each of you. You can choose what color you want, though."

"Red," said Philippa.

"Blue, I think," said Libby.

"Red and blue make purple," said Abba.

"A royal color, at any rate," murmured Mrs. Barber.

"Why not?" said Philippa. "A purple bathtub would be far-out." She began to warm up to the idea of the new house. Maybe they ought to invite everybody they knew to show off this place, have a real ball!

She tried out the idea on her father when they were alone together that evening. "Can we have a party when we move in? You know, a housewarming, and invite friends, and have a band, like when the Jolliffes celebrated Bat Mitzvah for Susan?"

Her father seemed a little alarmed. "Don't you think we ought to try this out first? We might want to ease into things. We'll have a few friends for dinner, the Jolliffes, of course, because Roy works with us. This is a working building, Flip, and we all have to work at making the whole deal work, at least in the beginning."

Philippa stared at her father. He was supposed to be in love with Libby's mother, and he sounded like some banker concluding a business deal. It was so tiring to think of nothing but work. "Listen," she said, "what do you two need Libby and me here for if it's such a lot of TS for everybody?"

"TS? Oh, oh!" Her father grinned more like his old self.

Philippa said, "You think, maybe, we're cogs in some big office machine. You'd probably call it Family Processing."

Her father laughed. Philippa reveled in the old closeness. He said, "To tell the truth, this emphasis on work is only a cover-up for anxiety, my anxiety, Janet's, yours, Libby's, too, I'll bet, though she never shows it. Let me tell you a secret."

"But that's why I want a party. I'm tired of secrets."

"This is a nice one. Janet and I have had our Wassermanns, the blood test you have to have before you can get a marriage license. We'll be ready when and if."

"Oh, no!" said Philippa.

"Then we'll celebrate," said her father.

"I can wait," said Philippa.

The next afternoon after school, Philippa went to Jane's. In the kitchen, making sandwiches with Jane, Philippa said, "This lovey-dovey stuff I've been telling you about? It's really happened. I have to move my things on Saturday to the apartment. I have to live by the old railroad sidings and the lumberyard."

Jane whistled. "I never thought you'd do it."

"They did it, not me."

"How can you leave your grandparents? Will I ever miss you!" Jane stopped spreading peanut butter on her slice of bread. She examined Philippa. Philippa vigorously spread jelly on the peanut-buttered slices.

"And what else?" Jane said. "You haven't told me the rest. I can tell."

"What else is there? Isn't it enough I got to live with those people? I have a new room, but I share a bath with Libby."

Jane tittered. "You'll love that! Go on."

"Jane, that's it, except for minor details."

"One minor detail has to be the wedding. When does that happen?"

"It doesn't. Mrs. Barber doesn't want any long-term commitments, she says." Philippa spread jelly back and forth, back and forth, on the same piece of bread.

"Wow!" said Jane.

"Let's finish these sandwiches before the kids come in," said Philippa.

After a while Jane said, "Sociologically speaking, they're kind of advanced, I think. That's what Mindy'd say. Can I tell Mindy? My mom?"

"Why not? Libby and I have to give Miss Hurholtz our new address. Everybody'll know we've moved."

"Hmp, your father and Libby's mom shacking up together!" Jane laughed.

Philippa poked Jane with the jelly knife. "This is serious business," she said.

The morning of the move, Philippa's father beckoned Philippa into his old room. The closet and drawers were empty, but everything else remained. He and Mrs. Barber had bought new bedroom furniture. "I want you to take this." Her father held the picture of Philippa's mother in its silver frame. "It's yours now." He kissed Philippa on the forehead. "Take care of it for me."

Philippa placed it in a duffel bag. Carrying the duffel in one hand and clasping the aquarium against her chest, she went downstairs.

On the porch, she kissed Abba and Pop once more. She got into the car beside her father, the aquarium balanced on her lap. They drove away.

Part II

AT 102 COMMERCE STREET

14

At 102 Commerce Street, Philippa stepped slowly out of the car. Water was not pouring from the statue yet, but its nudity was polished. The sidewalk was swept.

Her father charged up the outer steps with the aquarium that he'd taken from her lap and a suitcase. He set down the case under a new brass doorbell plate with a little holder that showed, freshly typed, BARBER/CATLETT.

Her father rang the bell in a noisy staccato, then flung the door open. "Welcome to 102 Commerce Street," he said.

"Hello! We were getting lonesome," said Mrs. Barber. She kissed Philippa's father and turned to Philippa. Philippa held the duffel bag in front of her so Libby's mother could not get too close.

"Do you need help unpacking?" asked Mrs. Barber.

"No! Uh, thanks," said Philippa. She started upstairs. Her father followed with her belongings.

"Libby is up there, I think. If you want anything, I am in the kitchen," called Mrs. Barber.

Philippa's father set the suitcase at Philippa's door and carefully handed over the aquarium. Then he practically ran downstairs.

Philippa kicked open the door to her room. For a moment she allowed herself to admire it. She loved the odor of fresh paint and the warm metal smell from the new radiator.

Mrs. Barber had designed a special shelf for her aquarium. It was painted deep sea-green and had its own electrical outlet. Philippa eased the tank onto the shelf and plugged in the aquarium light and bubbler. "Perfect fit, fishes," she said.

She looked down into the rear garden and wondered if Frisk might find his way here. Then she unsnapped the duffel bag. Mixed in with the socks was the photograph of her mother. She propped it on the windowsill. "There are no trees in back," Philippa said. "I hope you'll get used to the difference."

She went to inspect the bathroom. The tiles and shower curtain were lavender. Shocking magenta and royal purple towels hung on silver racks. "Out of sight," murmured Philippa. She noted that Libby's door was closed, and closed her own behind her.

The first school morning in the new house, Philippa

banged doors and shouted because Libby was using the shower when she wanted it. She was so noisy they heard her in the kitchen. Philippa's father had to stop Mrs. Barber from going to Libby's rescue. "They'll work it out," he said. "They can learn from one another."

From the very beginning Philippa was bothered by the way Libby said "George" to Philippa's father. "George, do you like my vegetable curry?" And another time, as Libby did ballet steps in the middle of the living room, she said, "George, let me hold your shoulder a minute."

Philippa ground her teeth. "Jaw-urge this and Jaw-urge that," she muttered. She could not bring herself to address Libby's mother as "Janet."

On the third evening in the new apartment, Philippa needed help preparing for a math quiz. She gave Libby the book and asked her to check answers for her, but Libby took forever looking for numbers that were right in front of her. Philippa grabbed the book. "Oh, never mind," she said. "You don't know anything!" She ignored the tears in Libby's blue eyes and bolted into the living room. Her father and Mrs. Barber were watching TV.

"Jaw-urge!" shouted Philippa. "I need help with my math quiz!"

"Say, just whom are you yelling at?" said her father.

Mrs. Barber held up a hand and said, "George, would you please see if I put the dishwasher on? I may have forgotten." Her father went. As she watched him go, Philippa's throat had a surprising ache.

"Sit with me, Philippa," said Mrs. Barber as she took a seat on the couch by the fireplace. "Show me the book. Are there questions you need help with?" She was very calm.

Philippa explained. At first her voice was gruff. As she went on, and Mrs. Barber seemed to understand a lot, Philippa asked about a problem not completed in class. Mrs. Barber showed her how to do it. She said, "You must be in an advanced math class."

"Yes, Libby doesn't do this yet."

Mrs. Barber smiled. "No, math is not Libby's strong subject. Any time you need help, be sure to ask me."

"Sure," said Philippa. Mrs. Barber, up close, smelled like lilacs and cinnamon.

"I mean, thank you," said Philippa, and she swung up the stairs as if she were a kite rising on a breeze.

Philippa knocked on Libby's door. "Come in," said a muffled voice. Philippa went in. Libby was lying on her bunk, one arm thrown across her face.

Philippa said, "Your mother helped me. She's real good. I'm sorry I got mad at you. You want to make some cinnamon toast? I'm hungry."

"Oh, yes!" said Libby, sitting up. "That would be lovely!"

15

"I see you have moved to the same address," said Miss Hurholtz when Philippa and Libby told her about 102 Commerce Street.

"That will be nice, to live so near one another. An apartment house, I suppose?"

"No," said Libby.

"Yes," said Philippa.

Miss Hurholtz smiled, waiting.

Philippa said, "It's a very small apartment house for only two families."

"Except we're practicing being one," said Libby.

"How interesting," said Miss Hurholtz.

"My father's office is in the building," said Philippa, "and Mrs. Barber works there, too, so it's more efficient for everybody to live there." Libby nodded.

"I am sure it will be fun for you both," said Miss Hurholtz. "Good luck in your new home." She called the class to order.

"Is it really fun," asked Jane after class, "the way Miss Hurholtz said? Or is it an incredible mess, like?"

"Sometimes it's awful," said Philippa, "but Libby's mother says it's challenging. Can you come see for yourself . . . sleep over Friday night?"

"Probably," said Jane. "You got to show me everything."

On Friday afternoon, Jane, Libby, and Philippa got off the bus at the corner of Commerce and Hennepin. "My dad operates that crane over there," Jane said as they passed a house with its side gone. "He says your parents were smart to move here while prices are still cheap."

Jane admired the cathedral ceiling of the living room and its skylight. "Costs a mint to heat," she said.

"No, not quite." Mrs. Barber had opened the front door and entered after them. "The skylight lets in sun. You must be Jane. I've heard so much about you. It's time we met." They shook hands.

"You are home early, Mother," said Libby.

"I wanted to greet our guest. It seems so unwelcoming to walk into an empty apartment. I'm going to turn the oven on before I go back to the office. Be sure to put in that baking dish on the counter when the oven light goes off."

"Sounds like home," Jane said. "I'll remember."

After Mrs. Barber left, Jane said, "How pretty your

mom is. How come neither of you ever said how pretty she is?"

Libby was pleased. "I'm going to tell her you said so."

Philippa sucked her cheeks. She said, "I guess my father wouldn't like somebody ordinary. C'mon. I want to show you my room."

After dinner, Philippa's father said, "Listen, kids, do you mind if we go to the Jolliffes' for a while?"

"Don't worry about a thing," said Jane. "I am used to baby-sitting. I keep calm under every circumstance."

Mrs. Barber giggled. "Jane, dear, things have settled down around here, but you may have to exercise diplomacy."

"Aw," said Philippa. "You don't have to treat us like babies. Can we play flashlight tag in the offices?"

"Be sure to lock up," said her father.

They played flashlight tag in the darkened offices till Philippa bruised her shin on a filing cabinet. Then Libby put the lights on so they could work the office machines. They made photocopies of pictures that they drew, and Philippa realized she had not had any desire to draw a Bibby Larber cartoon in a long time.

Afterward, they climbed the four flights of stairs to the bedrooms at the top of the house. Jane was panting. "Now I got to climb into the top bunk? You need an elevator."

Libby came through the shared bath and tucked herself on the foot of Philippa's bunk. "It's lonesome in there," she said. There was silence. Jane yawned. Philippa thrust her feet down where Libby sat. Libby made a spot as warm as Jack used to.

Jane said suddenly, "Wait till she gets pregnant."

"Wha-a-a-a-at?" said Philippa. She sat up and bumped her head on the bunk above it. It hurt.

"People take pills not to have babies," said Libby.

Jane rustled as she turned over. "People can decide different if they want to."

"There isn't any room here for more children," said Libby. "My mother has me."

"Yeah," said Philippa, "and she has me, and my father." She wondered why she was so angry.

"I'm beat," said Jane. "I wish you two'd shut up— thinking of yourselves all the time."

Libby unfolded herself from the bottom bunk and left, but when Philippa was almost asleep, she was startled by a body crawling into place beside her. Libby's quilt flopped into her face. "I am sorry if I disturbed you," Libby said, "but I have too much to think about to be by myself. I'll sleep in here tonight, if you don't mind."

Philippa rolled toward the wall to leave space for a second body. " 'Kay," she mumbled. The bunk was wide enough for two, anyway.

16

On the bus to school Monday morning, Libby said to Philippa, "That was fun having Jane. Whom shall we invite next weekend?"

"I could ask Laurie if you want," said Philippa. "It's your turn to ask next, though." She pushed through people to get to the rear of the bus.

"Excuse me, excuse me," Libby kept saying, until she caught up with Philippa. "Let's have Laurie, and then I'll invite Robin."

While they were waiting for the first bell in the school corridor, Philippa asked Laurie. "Sure, I'd love to," said Laurie. "I'll call you after I ask Mom."

After school, Philippa was due at home to clean. She began by initialing the cleaning schedule in the kitchen. That was the wrong order of doing things. Only after she had completed a job was she supposed to initial the posted schedule that Libby's mother had pinned up.

The house had too many schedules, Philippa thought: for laundry, for emptying trash, for cooking and shopping and cleaning. For a while, Philippa's father had said they were "testing the system for weak spots, like the Navy on a shakedown cruise."

Philippa had groaned and said, "And I'm seasick. I'll throw up if I see another schedule."

The phone rang as she was mopping the kitchen floor. Philippa was glad for the interruption. "Barber-Catlett residence," she said into the receiver.

"It's me, Laurie."

"Hi. You coming Friday?"

"I don't know. Maybe not. Mom went out to think. I mean, she's thinking while she's shopping."

"What's to think about?" said Philippa.

"Maybe my cousin's coming to visit," said Laurie, "or I'm going there. Mom said to tell you."

"Oh. How about next week?"

"Uh, I guess not."

"How do you know if you haven't asked yet? Ask and call me, okay?"

"Welllll. I better not. If my cousin doesn't come here, and I go there, then she'll come here next weekend, or I'll go there if she hasn't come here. I mean I got to go now. G'bye." Click.

Philippa looked at the dead phone. Something was wrong. Laurie was such a lousy liar.

Philippa forgot what she was doing and walked over the wet part of the floor, leaving dirty footprints. She had to mop them again and felt it was all Laurie's fault for being such a—but she did not know what Laurie was being. I'll find out tomorrow, Philippa promised herself.

The next day, Philippa tried to worm more information out of Laurie. "I just can't come," said Laurie.

"Oh, come on," said Philippa. "You know you want to see this place. It's so different, it's terrific. I have bunk beds and a built-in desk and shelves. Wait till you see our purple bathroom."

Laurie twisted a lock of hair around and around her forefinger. In a small voice, she said, "I don't want to."

"Why?"

Laurie started to leave. Philippa held on to her jacket pocket. Laurie looked as if she wanted to cry. "My mother doesn't, doesn't, doesn't w-want me in that neighborhood. She says maybe it isn't safe after d-dark."

"Sure, it's safe. After dark, there's nobody moved in yet but us. We can play flashlight tag in my father's office the way we did with Jane. It's fun and spooky. Tell your mother."

Laurie shook her head. "My mother won't let me go to your house. She says she doesn't like what goes on in it." Laurie jerked away. Her pocket ripped.

Philippa yelled, "What do you think goes on, stupid?"
Laurie was running like a deer.

Philippa was insulted. She buttonholed Carol, the next
person out the door. Philippa said, "Want to come sleep
over Friday night?"

Carol rolled her eyes. The corners of her mouth
twitched. She put a hand up to hide it, but Philippa could
see her eyes had the kind of superior smile that gave the
smiled-at person the jitters. Philippa's lower lip began to
stick out. Carol said, a little breathy, "Not this weekend.
Later, maybe?"

Philippa could hardly wait for her father and Libby's
mother to get home that night. She had to tell them about
Laurie and Laurie's mom. And about Carol's trying not to
laugh. "Hey!" Philippa announced. "Laurie's mom won't
let her sleep over Friday night. Carol was about to have
a pissy-fit when I asked her instead."

Philippa's father got steely-eyed. "What did Laurie's
mother say? Did she tell you?"

"Oh, some junk about this neighborhood not being
safe, the way Abba worries. But it was more what she said
after, about her mother not liking what went on in our
house. What does she mean, what goes on in our house
that's so different from anybody's house?"

Philippa's father turned to Libby's mother, who was
about to carry out the trash. In a hard voice he said, "Suppose Ma is right? This town is going to take it out on the
kids. Maybe it's already happening."

"What's happening?" said Philippa.

"Don't overreact to one report," said Libby's mother. She left with the big bucket for the outside container.

Philippa's father donned an apron, because it was his night to cook dinner. Then he went to the door and yelled after Libby's mother, "You want to bet? They're going to ostracize them because we are not meeting the town norms." He stood in the cold on the deck and waved his arms at Mrs. Barber down below.

"What's the matter with him?" said Philippa.

"They're starting their first fight," said Libby. "I hate it when parents fight, don't you?"

"How do I know?" said Philippa. She had never seen her father act this way.

"I'm going to do homework," said Libby. "Please help me with math, Philippa." Libby tugged at Philippa's sweater.

"We can work at the kitchen table," said Philippa. She had to keep track of what was going on.

"I'd rather do it upstairs."

Philippa's father slid the door open to let Libby's mother enter the kitchen ahead of him. He tried to grab the empty trash bucket. Libby's mother glared at him and held on. "You see, Mr. Know-it-all. I told you that's how you'd act if we got married. Possessive, possessive, *possessive!*"

"Hell, I'm just helping," said Philippa's father, "and it's important to give kids stability and a good home life."

Mrs. Barber's voice went high and shrill. "They have

stability and home life. It's you who are upsetting everyone." She put the bucket under the sink with an extra bang, then turned to face Philippa's father. Philippa noticed, wide-eyed, that Mrs. Barber had her fists clenched. These adults acted just like children!

"I don't want people sneering at my daughter." Philippa's father sounded nasty. His hands rested on his hips, and his knuckles looked knotty.

"Nobody's sneering at me," said Philippa. Libby had her hands over her ears.

"It's just like some self-righteous male booby to worry about what insignificant people think. Well, I am a person, and you can worry about what I think if I am significant to you, otherwise . . ."

Philippa's father tried to hold Mrs. Barber. She pushed him away with her hands on his chest. Philippa's father folded her hands up and kissed them, then when she kicked him in the shins, he yelled, "Bitch!" and landed a crooked kiss in a corner of her mouth.

Libby whispered, "We should give them time to settle things. Please, Philippa, come away." Libby nudged Philippa toward the stairs.

Philippa kept trying to see over Libby's shoulder, but Libby steadily pushed her to the top floor. Philippa hung over the railing to listen. A chair slammed over in the kitchen. Then there was silence.

Libby heaved a breath of what Philippa took to be relief. "They'll make up, and then it will be all right."

"Is that the way your mother and father acted?"

"Worse. When they threw things, Mother got the divorce."

"Is this the kind of stuff Laurie's mom doesn't like Laurie to be around? I didn't know your mother'd get mad so fast, especially at Dad."

"Mother's temper is very short when she feels her rights are being, you know, stepped on."

"Um, Dad was asking for it, I guess, but your mother fights okay."

"Oh, Phil-lip-puh!"

"You sound like Abba."

"You sound like such a child!"

"Well, I like that! I'm older than you are by three months."

Dinner was late that evening. Both Philippa's father and Libby's mother seemed to have little appetite. Philippa would have liked to continue the conversation with her father but thought better of it. The fight may have been interesting, but she could not face another so soon. Even being a watcher was rather exhausting. Instead, she and Libby played a game of Othello on the rug in the living room. Their eyes met over the board whenever Mrs. Barber talked to Philippa's father and vice versa. Even though the adults sounded ordinary, there was an electric undercurrent.

At nine o'clock, without prompting, Philippa and Libby climbed the stairs to their rooms. Philippa held back so

Libby could go first around the curve where the steps narrowed. In the shared bath, they brushed their teeth side by side at their double sink. Then they went into their own rooms, and that night, they left both doors to the bathroom open wide.

17

Walking Jane home for old times' sake the next afternoon, Philippa asked, "What's up with Laurie? Carol, too."

Jane looked at Ted and Amber and Denise and said to Amber, "I wonder who can run the fastest to the Civil War Monument."

When they were out of hearing, Jane said, "They're too little to understand."

"Understand what?" said Philippa.

"You know. How your father and Libby's mother are living together. Some people laugh about it, so their kids do, too."

"What's so funny?"

"It's not what ordinary grown-ups do in this town. They get married. They don't just move in together."

"Dad and Libby's mother had a fight when I asked

about Laurie and Carol. I think Mrs. Barber won. I don't see why anybody but Abba cares. She's in love with weddings. Is everybody?"

Jane shrugged. "Beats me, but weddings are usual. It's exciting to talk about what's unusual, isn't it? Where I baby-sit sometimes on Saturday night . . . they were talking over drinks. One lady said it's 'flaunting sex-u-al-ity.' Isn't that wild?" She looked sidewise at Philippa.

"Is that what your mother says?"

"Of course not. My mother says it's none of our business what people do as long as they don't hurt anybody."

Philippa said, "I'll fight anybody who makes fun of us. I'll lambaste 'em from here to Commerce Street." She beat one hand into the palm of the other.

"If it'd do any good, I'd bop the whole class for you, Phil. I think Mindy'd say violence doesn't settle anything. Maybe you ought to invite more kids for sleepovers so they see there's nothing weird in your house, only people living there."

"But Laurie said her mom won't let her come, and Carol was laughing when I asked her."

"Those are only one kind of people. Ask some of the others. Not everyone thinks the same way. Some kids accept the way you are, and some just laugh at what's different from them."

Philippa said, "I'm not sure what you just said. Say it again."

"I mean it," said Jane. "Adults are the same way. I think

they get uncomfortable with exceptionals. *I* am an exceptional."

"Oh," said Philippa. "Me, too. Thanks, Jane," and she ran for her bus. It was her afternoon to vacuum the bedrooms.

On the second floor, Philippa tugged the vacuum by its hose to give a lick and a promise to the upper hallway. There was a whoosh, and the motor became agitated. The suction disappeared. She'd sucked up something bigger than usual. "Hell's bells," said Philippa. She twisted off the hose.

"Hello." The door opened and shut down below. Libby was home from ballet class.

Philippa yelled down the stairs. "Bring the ice tongs. They're hanging by the refrigerator."

After a moment, Libby appeared. She had a duffel bag in one hand, the ice tongs in the other. "Whatever do you want these for?" she said.

Gingerly, Philippa lifted the hose as though it were a boa constrictor. "It's plugged up with something."

Libby poked the tongs into the hose and drew out a limp bundle. As she held it by its shoulder straps, they could see the prongs had left holes in a flimsy, very short slip. Runs blossomed up and down from the prong punctures. "Oh, dear. It's one of Mother's camisoles," said Libby. "You've ruined it."

"*I* ruined it! You poked it full of holes so it—"

"You told me to use the tongs."

"How can I keep my cleaning schedule with a stuffed-up vacuum? I'd like to know how come your mother leaves a, a kama sole on the floor anyhow. You'd think she'd be more private with her underwear."

"Maybe your father dropped it."

"Poo, Dad wouldn't wear—" Philippa stopped. Was she ever a dope. She looked at Libby, then at the garment. It was very pretty. She reached out to touch it. It was soft and creamy.

"I can't wait to be old enough to wear one," Libby said.

"It doesn't cover much," Philippa said. "I mean, you can almost see through it. You'd freeze to death."

"It's for shape, not warmth." Libby examined the camisole thoughtfully. "Philippa, now that they've made up their fight, I think it might be best if we throw this away, not return it, ruined, and then, you know, I have to explain, and you have to explain, and they have to explain, and—" Libby flipped the camisole in a gesture of helplessness.

"I'll hide it in my trash." Philippa crushed the camisole to a handful and went into her room. She threw it under crumpled papers in her wastebasket. She'd remember to empty it even if it wasn't her turn on the schedule.

18

The following morning Philippa sneezed six times in a row. "I think I'm going to bed," she said. Her throat was scratchy.

Libby, who was washing her face at the other sink, dried it quickly and said, "I'll get Mother."

"Don't want anybody," said Philippa, crawling under the covers. She felt hot and cold at the same time.

Mrs. Barber's hand was cool on her forehead. "Open your mouth," she said. "Let's see if you have a temperature." The thermometer slid under Philippa's tongue. Philippa closed her eyes again. Her head ached, and she wished Mrs. Barber would leave her hand on her forehead.

Mrs. Barber removed the thermometer and stepped to the window to check it. "Hm," she said. "One hundred and one. Are you coughing?"

Philippa forced a cough. "My throat hurts, and I sneeze too much."

Mrs. Barber gave the thermometer to Libby, who kept hovering. "Sweetie, please wash the thermometer for me."

Mrs. Barber returned to Philippa and sat on the edge of the bunk. I'm going to bring you a light breakfast," she said, "and an aspirin. You are in no condition to go to school."

"It's overwork," said Libby from the bathroom doorway.

Mrs. Barber frowned. "What do you mean?" she said.

Libby returned the thermometer to its blue case and gave it to her mother. "Why, it's scrub this, wash that, dust the furniture, vacuum the floor, mop the tiles, empty the trash. Philippa and I never have any fun. The first time we even had anybody here to *talk* to was when Jane came that weekend. It's not fair, and now Philippa is sick."

"A cold is a virus," said Mrs. Barber. "You have to catch a germ," but she seemed thoughtful.

She went downstairs and when she returned with a tray, Mrs. Barber sat in the red beanbag chair. Philippa chewed halfheartedly at a slice of toast. "Do you feel overworked the way Libby says?" asked Mrs. Barber.

"I s'pose," said Philippa. "Maybe you and Dad like this working jag. There's not much in it for Libby and me, is there?"

Mrs. Barber pulled at her lower lip. "Maybe I have been forgetting you children. I'm sorry. There has been so much to do at the office, and I have not paid enough attention to what you two have done here. I'll look for a cleaning service to do the floors and the heaviest work." She took away the tray, and soon after, Philippa's father appeared.

"Under the weather?" he said. He sat down as best he could on the edge of the bottom bunk and held her hand. "Janet and I will take turns coming to visit you today. She is unhappy because she thinks we have forgotten to work at being a family together, and that's bad, because that's why we're here together in the first place."

"More work," said Philippa.

Her father chuckled. "You know we both love you. There doesn't seem to have been much time to show it. When you get well, we'll have a genuine family outing, okay?"

"Sure," said Philippa. She sneezed.

Mrs. Barber kept Philippa home a second day. "You need one day at home without a fever," she said.

"What am I going to do here alone?" wailed Philippa. She felt fine, only blew her nose long and loudly.

"Come down to the office. I have some filing you can do. You can answer phones when Mrs. Fargo goes to lunch."

"Hey!" said Philippa. "Neat."

She had such a good time working, Philippa forgot the promised family outing. She did not think of it until the event was announced for the weekend, an evening of ice-skating at the newly built indoor rink. Libby was ecstatic, but Philippa groaned. "Maybe I'll have a fever again," she said.

"You don't like ice-skating?" said Libby. Her blue eyes crinkled with concern.

Philippa filled her mouth with baked potato so she did not have to answer immediately. She was a good swimmer, not bad at basketball, and a terrific field-hockey player. But ice-skating was a pain. Her ankles bent inward, and she hobbled around the next day with shooting pains up and down her shins. Libby was still looking at her.

Philippa remembered how Libby had spoken up about their having to work too hard, and how they'd spent a great weekend sharing Jane, and she just could not say, "I hate ice-skating."

Instead, she swallowed her food and said, "It's not my best sport, but I'll go."

In spite of her doubts, Philippa dressed carefully for the occasion. She put on her dove-gray cords and her best wine-berry and gray shirt. She was pleased at the way her hair shone and the pants fit sleek over her rump . . . tighter than Abba had ever allowed. She was more than satisfied with her grown-up looks. At least she was until she caught sight of Libby through the bathroom door.

Libby was dressed for the Olympics. She wore a navy-blue skating costume. It had a fitted top fastened with tiny velvet buttons. The skirt was so short it revealed miles of Libby's slender legs in blue tights. Besides, the skirt was trimmed with bunny fur, and the muff that was hung on a cord from her neck must have been bunny fur also.

Philippa watched as Libby picked up a brocade bag with a white zipper down one side. Libby bent close to her mirror to smile at herself, then, without a glance in Philippa's direction, she skipped out her door.

Philippa felt as dowdy as Babbitt in Paris. That was one of her grandmother's phrases, and for the first time in her life, Philippa understood it.

First to get in the car, Libby beamed at everyone. "I am so happy to be skating again." A cartoon flashed into Philippa's head. It was a skater like Libby taking a pillow out of a brocade bag and strapping it to her bottom in case of falls.

Mrs. Barber came out of the brownstone last. She was dressed in jeans and a ski jacket. Her eyes sparkled under a ski cap, which had confined her hair to a few curls that escaped around the edges. She never managed to look old enough to be anybody's mother. Jane would have said she was very pretty.

As they drove out on Route 136, Libby bubbled with skating stories. "And I haven't skated since my figure-skating lessons last year," she said. No wonder they were going ice-skating, thought Philippa. And where did that leave her? An outsider again, that's where!

Philippa's father parked the car, and they walked to the swinging glass doors in a big oval building. There was a neon sign, DISKO-SKATE. Philippa's father pushed open a door for everyone to enter.

At first Philippa was appalled by the cavernous darkness and the blare of sound. Then she focused on the colored spotlights. They were dizzily reflected from two whirling glass spheres, bigger than volleyballs, hung from the ceiling at either end of the arena. The balls were diamonded with tiny mirrors.

Philippa's father rented skates for everyone except Libby. The rented skates were tan suede with red numbers on the heels. From the brocade bag, Libby brought out a pair of gleaming white leather skates with pink rubber blade protectors. "My father had them custom made," she said.

Libby laced the skates swiftly and stood without a wobble. "Coming, Philippa? I'll teach you a figure eight."

"I'm not ready. I don't think these skates fit right." Philippa stamped her feet in the skates and yanked at one shoelace. It was too strong to break.

"Let me help you," said Mrs. Barber. She knelt in front of Philippa and began lacing the skates. It was clear that they fit. Laced into the skates, Philippa clumped to the swinging gate that led from the changing area to the rink. She watched the flow of bodies swirling around and around on the ice.

Every skater had to move in the same direction. When bells chimed, everyone turned and skated in the opposite direction. Philippa thought the ice on Hadley's Meadow, when the Fire Department flooded it, was more fun than this decorated place. The roar of the music was enough to give you a headache.

"Don't be afraid, Philippa. I'll skate with you while you

get used to the skates." Libby, hands in muff, had sneaked up beside her.

No reasonable person would accept help from someone in that weirdo outfit! "I can't hear you," yelled Philippa. "The music's too loud," and she made herself break into the river of people and skate away fast.

Philippa worked her way toward the middle of the arena. She saw that one could practice there in the calm center. When she arrived, she was dismayed to see that Libby was already there, twirling like a top so fast she was a blur. Arms outstretched, skirt rippling out from her body, Libby flipped around on her toe blades, then, carving a semicircle of shaved ice, she came to a halt. "Did you see me, Philippa? That's the first time I've done that this year."

"I can skate backwards," said Philippa. At least, Jane had tried to teach her last year on a trip to Hadley's Meadow. She began to stroke, keeping her head turned to see over her shoulder.

"Use your hips a little more," advised Libby. "Like this." She swung into a fluid motion that carried her backwards. Imagine showing off all the time, Philippa thought.

"I'm going to get a soda," said Philippa. She got to a gate and thumped to the snack bar, ankles falling inward and already aching, and ordered a root beer. She wondered how long it would take to learn to do a spin the way Libby did.

Philippa returned to the rink. She struck out to see

where her father had gotten to. There. Between bodies, Philippa saw him with an arm around Mrs. Barber's waist. They skated side by side. Her father glanced down, and Mrs. Barber lifted her face up, as if no one else existed. This was family togetherness?

Philippa, regardless of her flopping ankles, pushed hard to catch up. She thought to plunge between them and shove them apart. With her head down, Philippa did not see them veer right. She sped through empty space. It was like stepping onto a stair that was not there. She stopped, bewildered. Behind her, her father and Mrs. Barber called and waved.

Philippa had to keep straight on. That was the rule of the place. Disgruntled, Philippa jostled skaters this way and that. A staid skater in a green uniform wagged a finger at her. "Watch yourself," the rink guard said. "Skate under control at all times."

Philippa slid to a railing to catch her breath. She leaned against it, limp as a mop hung up to dry.

"There you are, Philippa. I came to see how you are enjoying the ice." Philippa stiffened. Mrs. Barber'd caught her before she'd had a chance to leave the rink.

"Isn't it marvelous?" Mrs. Barber asked. Philippa shrugged.

Then the music changed. It went so soft and gentle it gave Philippa a sadness between her ribs. "Ah," said Mrs. Barber, "I love that old 'Skaters' Waltz.' Do you know how to cross wrists and skate together? It's old-fashioned and fun." She reached for Philippa's left hand with her right.

Reluctantly, Philippa extended a glove. Her father swooped in front of them and reached for Philippa's right hand.

They were skating, the three of them, hip to hip. Philippa's wrists were crossed, and her hands were held firmly from both sides. She could not falter. Caught in the waltz, she swept smoothly around the rink. The whirly glass balls revolved their lights. Stroke this way. Stroke that way. Close together. Slide. And slide.

Philippa closed her eyes. She was close between a mother and a father.

Somewhere, far off and somewhere else, she had once before known this between feeling. Philippa opened her eyes and was dazzled a moment by a whorl of a storm of —snowflakes? "Oh!" said Philippa. Fear squeezed her heart. Snowflakes . . . tumbling over and over in the dark . . . flashing lights . . . a scream . . . hers.

But she need not scream. The light patterns fell harmlessly about her, rainbow diamonds, not snow.

Philippa took a deep breath and knew she was safe.

The music ended. This skating session was closing, and a machine would sweep the ice. The three skated to a gate. "Thank you both," said Mrs. Barber. "I enjoyed that very much."

"Me, too," said Philippa's father.

Philippa licked her lips. They had become very dry.

"Guess it's time to go home," said her father. The evening was over. Philippa could relax. In the car she savored again that feeling of being safe between.

"It has been a lovely evening," said Mrs. Barber at the

Commerce Street curb. "I bought a jug of cider earlier today. I'm going to make a special drink—mulled cider."

Philippa climbed the stairs and entered the kitchen without a word.

As they sat around the table her father said, "You're very quiet tonight, Flip."

"I'm thinking," said Philippa, and buried her nose in the steaming cup.

As if she thought Philippa now loved skating, Libby said, "I know," and smiled her most maddening, knowing smile.

Philippa got cross-eyed staring down along the cinnamon stick in her hot cider. No, you don't, she thought. You really don't. You weren't there, between.

19

In a few more weeks there were grackles circling with the street pigeons and redwings calling in the swampy place by the railroad siding. Spring had come to 102 Commerce Street.

One Saturday morning Philippa's father strode around the rear garden measuring for seed beds. Philippa held one end of the tape. "Tomatoes in the middle," he said. "They need full sun. Lettuce there, and we can plant it early."

"I want bushels of flowers," said Mrs. Barber.

"I love planning a garden," said Libby.

"We have to buy seeds and equipment," said Philippa's father. "We're lucky the lumberyard stocks everything." They walked to Forello's Lumber & Hardware. They discovered they needed a wheelbarrow, a spade, a rake, trowels, and fertilizer. The salesman suggested a barbecue grill on red wheels, and then four canvas folding chairs seemed like a good idea.

Philippa's father rolled the wheelbarrow home. Piled with chairs and the bag of fertilizer, there was no room for the tools. Libby's mother and Libby divided the equipment between them. Philippa pushed the barbecue. They made a parade along Railroad Avenue, to Hennepin, down Hennepin to Commerce. Philippa's father had to help lift the barbecue down curbs and up again. In front of the boy fountain at 102 Commerce, he wiped his forehead in the crook of his arm and grinned. "I dunno," he said, "whether to feel *possessive* about all these *possessions*, or *trapped* by future considerations." He chuckled as if mightily amused.

Philippa knew he was making fun of the words Mrs. Barber had used. She looked at Libby, and Libby looked at Philippa. They both looked at Mrs. Barber. Surprisingly, she laughed. Then Philippa's father said, "We had another blood test. What do you think of that, kids?"

"You mean the one you have so you can get a marriage license?" asked Philippa.

"Yes."

Libby's mouth dropped open. She took a deep breath, but "You didn't" was all she said.

Mrs. Barber nodded and settled the tools more comfortably on her shoulder. "Please don't mention it to anybody, especially not to your grandmother, Philippa."

"Okay," said Philippa.

Philippa did not talk about it to Abba, nor to anybody, except, of course, to Jane—who wasn't just "anybody."

On Monday, over the din of the cafeteria, Philippa screamed into Jane's ear: "They're only thinking about it. It'll never happen. You don't know Mrs. Barber the way I know her. Only don't tell anybody."

They were crowded around a table so tightly that Robin Ehrlich, next to Jane, overheard. "Wouldn't it be great if the whole class got invited to the wedding?"

Said Philippa, "Shhh. There may never be one. Don't tell anybody, okay?"

"If there is a wedding, can I come, too?" said Laurie, who always seemed to be hanging around, wistful-like, where you least expected her.

"Oh, crapola!" said Philippa, beginning to perspire. "It's only rumor, see?" But she knew she'd blown it. She had talked about what she had been asked not to.

The next afternoon after class, Philippa volunteered to wash the chalkboard. When she finished, she lined up the erasers, beaten clean in the wastebasket, and remembered to get her sweater from the cloakroom. As she slid the door in its groove, she jumped a foot. There was a body huddled in a corner. "Libby?"

Libby sniffed. "Go awa-a-a-ay." Her shoulders heaved.

"It's me. Are you crying?"

"My Kleenex is soaked. You got any?" Philippa offered the tissue box from Miss Hurholtz's desk. Libby blew. She helped herself to another tissue.

Between wipes, she said, "If anybody else asks one more prying question, I will just kill them." Libby dabbed at her puffy eyes. "You're so lucky."

"Me? Lucky? People are already asking me for invitations to the wedding. I couldn't be unluckier. I'm the one that blabbed to Jane."

"You're so lucky because you can talk to your father. I can't talk to mine."

"I have change left from lunch," said Philippa. "Let's share a frosted at the Peppermint Box."

They sat in a corner booth and had a pineapple milk shake with vanilla ice cream with two straws, as ordered by Libby. Philippa preferred chocolate-mint, but you had to make concessions sometimes.

"When I was little," said Libby after a long pull at the straw, "we lived together, the three of us. I remember what it was like living with my father. He took me for walks late at night. I rode on his shoulders, piggyback. We were very happy when we were a family."

"Dad says we're happy together now," said Philippa. "Me, I don't think it's half bad, most of the time."

"No matter what happens, you don't have to change your name," said Libby. "I mean, it'll be you, and your father, and my mother will be a Catlett, too, and then there will be me, Libby Barber. I want my own name, but I don't want to be, you know, different."

"Different. Um." Philippa held her chin in her hands.

"After all, I love my father. Part of me belongs to him."
Libby looked at Philippa over the glass.

Libby made sense to Philippa, except that she had felt
she belonged totally to her father. But that wasn't completely true, she realized, because part of her also belonged
to Abba and Pop. Philippa hurried to get in a swallow of
the shake, then said, "Part of you can always belong to
your father, can't it?"

"Yes, but George is so sweet. I think I might love him,
too."

Philippa felt a twinge of envy. "So you'll have two
fathers. I'll never have more than one."

Libby went on, "Yes, but sometimes I think my life has
so many little pieces to it, I might just—explode."

"You look too solid to explode, skinny but solid."

Libby giggled. Her eyes seemed brighter. She gave one
last suck at her straw. It drew in the bubbles at the bottom. "I can't talk to Mother these days. She says the future
is making her nervous as a witch."

Philippa scraped the glass with her straw and slid her
tongue along it. Then she said, "Look, you won't change
any, even if your mother puts another one of those hyphens
in her name. You're still who you are. You have to be
yourself first and part of a family afterward. If kids at
school ask dumb questions, never mind. We can play it
cool, see, but you can talk to me, anytime."

20

From then on they stuck together at school like two halves of a clam. Philippa snapped, "Get off our case," if someone asked if the wedding date was set.

Libby only looked vague. "What are you referring to?" she said. "The event we are going to celebrate is Philippa's birthday, in June. With a barbecue. In the garden."

"We're not inviting any jerks either," said Philippa, "so stop acting like a jerk if you want to come."

Robin Ehrlich said yearningly, "My mother asks and asks about your mother. I say I haven't met her yet, and she says stop being shy."

"She is a working person," said Philippa. "Mrs. Barber is very busy."

"Don't you call her Mother or something?"

"Wouldn't you like to come for dinner Friday and stay

over?" said Libby sweetly. "We'd enjoy having you, wouldn't we, Philippa?"

"I guess," said Philippa.

Mrs. Ehrlich drove Robin to 102 Commerce Street after school on Friday. Robin carried an overnight bag, and Mrs. Ehrlich carried a cake. "This is a fabulous house!" said Mrs. Ehrlich. "Fantastic. Is your mother here?" she said to Philippa.

Philippa noticed it was a caramel-walnut cake, not chocolate. She frowned at Mrs. Ehrlich.

"She means Libby's mother," said Robin tactfully.

"Mother is an architect," said Libby. "We don't see her and George till dinner."

"This is a wonderful kitchen," said Mrs. Ehrlich, "so functional but so good-looking. I will go to her office and introduce myself, since I am president of our school PTA." She whisked out in a whirl of scarves.

"Ma says the way to get something done is to do it," said Robin, "before you get any older. That's how she is. Can I see the garden and your rooms and the skylights?"

First Libby slid the glass doors open to the deck above the garden. They climbed down to the patio paving. "I helped set these bricks," said Philippa.

Before dinner, Mrs. Barber asked the three girls to make the fruit salad. As Robin peeled an orange, she said, "This is what my mother thinks is so great . . . how you all work together."

"Your mother is a very persuasive woman," said Mrs.

Barber. "She invited me to speak at a PTA meeting on working mothers. Imagine me a public speaker!"

In a day or two, Janet Metz-Barber's picture appeared in the newspaper. Philippa noticed the photograph showed off her hair and figure quite well. In the article, Mrs. Paula Ehrlich, PTA President, announced a symposium on working mothers.

"What's a symposium?" said Philippa. She was standing with Robin, Libby, and some others on the playground after school.

"It's where they have a banquet, and then everyone talks," said Robin.

"They must be in sympathy with each other, I think," said Libby. "You know ... *sym*pathy ... *sym*posium ... ?"

"All this fuss about Mrs. Barber talking somewhere. I can hear her talk any old night." Philippa was aware of someone hanging at her elbow.

It was Laurie. "What do you want?" asked Philippa.

Silently, Laurie extended a handful of M&M's to Philippa, then passed the bag around the group. After a while Robin and Libby left for ballet class, but Philippa ate each tiny candy slowly, including Libby's uneaten portion. She knew Laurie was trying to buy back friendship now that Mrs. Barber was famous.

"We haven't talked in a long time," said Laurie.

Philippa sucked chocolate off a tooth. "So talk," she said. Philippa was not going to make it easy for some twerp who wouldn't even set foot inside her home.

Laurie's voice was small. "Robin said she stayed at your house last weekend."

"Sure. We had a good time. I'm asking Jennifer for next Friday."

Laurie's eyes were so eager, like a puppy's, but her mouth turned down. "My father said it's all right, I can come sometime."

It was too hard remaining mean and cold. Casually, Philippa said, "I haven't asked Jennifer yet. You want to come instead?"

"Oh, *yes*, I'll ask at home, but I'm sure it's okay."

It better be, thought Philippa, but her insides seemed to smile. "Call me tonight," she said, and grabbed at a swing to stand tall and pump and pump with a sudden spurt of energy. You could forgive an old friend almost anything.

That evening, Philippa sat beside Mrs. Barber on the sofa. In between questions about her math homework, she said, "Laurie's coming to stay Friday night."

"Fine, anyone you and Libby enjoy."

"At first, Laurie's parents wouldn't let her visit."

"Oh, I remember." Mrs. Barber nodded.

"But it's okay now."

"I hope so. Philippa, if your father and I have made life difficult for you and Libby at school, we really never meant to."

"Oh, wellll," said Philippa.

"Life has been hard for us sometimes, too. And me—I

couldn't have faced another marriage so soon. Can you understand that?"

"What's to understand?" said Philippa. "How we live is nobody's business, Dad says. It's our own life. I can handle the kids at school." At least she thought she could.

Mrs. Barber heaved a sigh—of relief, maybe? Philippa frowned, wondering. "You been worried about what *I* thought?"

"Of course. George and I have worked so hard at setting up this apartment, just to have both you girls with us. We want you to be happy because we need you."

This was pretty heavy conversation, Philippa thought. But if Mrs. Barber could give it out, she ought to be able to take it, too. Philippa looked Libby's little mother straight in the eye and said, "Yeah, sure, except parents get to do what they want. Kids don't."

Mrs. Barber did not flinch. "Children are supposed to do what parents think best, isn't that so? George and I have always discussed everything with you."

Philippa rubbed her nose. "Some parents can't make up their minds. Like Laurie's parents switched theirs. I think your picture in the paper did it. Huh!"

Mrs. Barber grinned. "Tell me, Philippa, given a choice right now, where would you most want to live?"

Philippa picked a raveling off her sweater and flicked it away. She said, "It's neat here."

"You didn't want to come at first, remember? I think

many people besides you need time to know what they want. Maybe that happened to Laurie and her parents."

Philippa considered this as she leaned closer to Libby's mother to turn a page of the math book lying in Mrs. Barber's lap. "I was explaining this lesson to you. You have to understand about negative and positive numbers. The tricky thing is when you multiply two negatives you get a positive. I don't know if you understand that."

Mrs. Barber smiled. "The way you put two girls like Libby and you together and get the right relationship."

"Listen," said Philippa firmly, "this is no joke. Now, look, when I multiply these two numbers with minus signs, I get a positive answer."

"Maybe it's like a double negative. If I say, I don't not like you, what do I mean?"

" 'I do like you.' " replied Philippa.

"I like you, too, Philippa." Mrs. Barber was laughing! Philippa resorted to Abba's voice: "See here, Janet, quit fooling around. Pay attention. *Minus* five, times *minus* five, is *plus* twenty-five. The numbers don't minus together the way you might expect. They make a *positive*, get it?"

Mrs. Barber ran a hand through her witchy curls. "Yes, just as this group of separate people has become a family —we're all plusses now." Mrs. Barber was still joking.

But then she grew serious. "You know, Philippa, it's nice when you say my own name. It makes me feel I mean something *positive* to you, too." She put her hand over Philippa's on the book.

Philippa left her hand where it was, but, "What are you talking about?" she said.

"I think of you as my daughter as well as Libby."

"Oh. That's okay," said Philippa, "if that's the way you want it." She had to squirm a little bit.

"I hoped you might want to be mine, too, but I'll settle for 'Janet,' anything besides 'Hey you.'"

It was Philippa's turn to grin, though she was half-embarrassed. "Tell you what, I'll promise to stop thinking of you as 'Libby's mother.'"

" 'Janet,' please."

"I'll promise to stop thinking of you as 'Libby's mother,' *Janet*."

"Thank you, Philippa."